I0517002

Greed, Golden Hair,
and
Green Eyes.

James Flynn

Annadale Press

ISBN: 0992783852
ISBN-13: 978-0-9927838-5-3

Annadale Press
26 Southcroft Road
London SW17 9TR

To Judy,
who was the first to read the manuscript,
and was kind enough to say she liked it.

CONTENTS

1 THE LODGER

She had been recommended to me by a friend of mine called Giles who knew her as a waitress at the Cafe Noir, a hang out for fake Bohemians and the sort of people who don't mind who hears their conversation.

"You have a spare room and you need the money. What more do you want?"

"Peace and quiet."

"I'm not asking you to marry her, just put her up for a couple of months."

"What's it to you?"

"Nothing, but if you do me this little favour, then I will have done her a little favour and," his eyes began to dream, "who knows? And don't forget, there is the rent."

"What's wrong with your place?"

"You know it's a studio flat, one room and, more to the point, one bed. I'm not ready for that kind of commitment yet. Besides, she turned me down."

A few days later she moved in and I could see why Giles liked her. Donetta was her name and she was like a petite Venus with a pale olive complexion, curly golden hair and green eyes. She had come over from Croatia a week or two before to study acting and she certainly had some of the qualifications. She was naturally noisy and dramatically temperamental.

She worked hard and, what with her shifts at the Noire and her acting classes, I rarely saw her. Occasionally, late at night, we would share some beer, or wine and talk. She was superstitious, interested in the occult and a teller of wild tales, yet even with all her overdone flamboyance and cynical disparagement of most people she was good company. In fact, her intelligence, her beauty and her rather too interested look whenever I said anything would have quickly put me under her spell, if I had not known my broken heart would make me immune.

One evening during a discussion on dark forces

which had been heavy on atmosphere but light on information, she leant forward conspiratorially and pointed to her finger. I refocused through a wine dark haze and stared. Her hands were small and shapely and looked as if they had never done a day's work in their lives.

"What's wrong? They look perfect."

She laughed. "Not the hands stupid, the ring."

I looked again. On the third finger of the right hand was a finely wrought ruby ring the colour of pigeon's blood.

"It is very special. Can you feel its power?

I stared harder. The dark red stone seemed to glow with a malign fire, but that was probably my imagination.

"Where did you get it?" I asked.

"It has a strange history. Someday, maybe I'll tell you."

She displayed the ring on her hand while her green eyes sparkled with the thrill of possession.

I assumed this was no more than a pleasant fantasy to add a touch of mystery and glamour and changed the subject by suggesting a brandy nightcap. Later, I thought I remembered making a pass at her, but it turned out she was the one who was immune.

The Peter Delaney Music Agency, which is me, has a second hand computer, an answer phone and a filing cabinet. With this technology at its disposal, it books ethnic acts from Europe and fallen stars from England and America into the art centre and club circuit. At the time everything was on the downslide except the phone bill.

One morning, not long after Donetta had moved in, Giles prized himself loose from the Cafe Noire and called over. His real name was McCready, but he called himself de Rais after the fifteenth century French occultist and murderer, Gilles de Rais. He felt it gave a 'dangerous edge of things' feel to his innocuous, esoteric songs and leant weight to his stage persona.

"Hello Giles."

"De Rais, if you don't mind. Is Donetta in?"

"She went out early this morning. Anything important?"

"No, someone was asking for her at the Noire. I really came to see you. You're my agent - remember?"

I led the way upstairs to the front room, which doubled as a living room and an office. De Rais collapsed on to the battered sofa in front of the genuine gas fire and appeared to go into a trance. I went back to the filing cabinet and continued looking for some publicity on a fiddle player from Norway. A few minutes passed.

"Any gigs coming in?"

I looked round and saw a gaunt face and a mass of light brown hair raised above the back of the sofa.

"What's wrong, the crystal stall at Camden not doing so well?"

"I haven't starved yet, but it's no thanks to you, I am supposed to be a musician."

I found the publicity, pulled it out, slammed the drawer and turned round.

"Giles - de Rais, you know the score. If I have got some Sixties throwback on my books and I phone up a venue and say do you want Old Joe Gallooly and the Daisies, they say: 'Great!' and all I have to do is send them a contract. On the other hand, if I ask them to book de Rais, the grave dark, mystical, moody, songwriter whose last album, 'Dance of Death', sold two hundred copies, their enthusiasm is more muted. They say: 'Even if he is as good as you say he is, can we get an audience?' I point out that they are an art centre and, therefore, have a budget. That's when they tell me that funds are a bit tight at the moment and to try again in April.

"All right," said Giles, "I know you have tried, but there must be something I can do, even if the masses are not ready for me yet."

"Of course I've tried, but then explaining all this de Rais stuff doesn't make it any easier. I feel like I've got one of the Moors' murderers on my books."

"Huh! You're like everybody else, afraid to look evil in the eye. You have to confront it, make it back down, with your visionary mind and dead man's stare."

"That's the best excuse I've heard yet for invoking a murderer in the name of money."

"The deadly de Rais favoured me with a sulky silence for a few minutes until I relented and gave him the good news.

"The 'Talking Dead' seance group in Fulham want you to open the show for them again. I managed to push them to £200 this time."

"When is that?"

"Halloween."

"Great, that cannot be more than a month away." He bounced out of the sofa and started pacing up and down the room.

"There must be other seances that need a bit of atmosphere to start the evening off. Maybe we could get a circuit going. Hey!..."

I looked up from trying to address an envelope and saw him staring out of the window.

"That bloke who was asking for Donetta" he hissed, "he is standing over the road."

I moved over to take a look. A tall, slim, dark haired figure was leaning against a bus stop on the other side of the road smoking a cigarette.

"He must have followed you" I said, "he is probably a friend from Croatia."

"I don't like it, I don't like it at all" muttered Giles.

"Why, what could be wrong?"

He turned his unhealthy pallor and dark rimmed eyes on me.

"He is too good looking, that's what's wrong."

I laughed. "Don't worry, I expect he is only her husband who has travelled half way across Europe to ask her to take pity on him and return to the children."

"Spare me your... Hold on! he is coming over."

The doorbell rang and I went down to answer it.

"Sorry to disturb you, but does Donetta Taveric live here?" He spoke with an East European accent.

"Yes, but she is out" I replied, "and I am not sure when she'll be back. Can I give her a message, or get her to phone you?"

"It does not matter, I will call again, either here or at the Noire. Could you tell her Ivan wishes to see her?"

I said I would and went back upstairs to find the great de Rais with his face pressed against the window trying to look sideways down the street at the retreating back.

"Well," he said, turning, "what do you make of that?"

"Nothing, my lodger knows someone called Ivan. What do you make of it, Holmes?"

Giles threw himself back onto the sofa, putting his boots up on one end and leaning his head against the other. "Something is not right" he said, "I can feel it. All the psychic auras around him are wrong. I knew it the first second I saw him. Still," he gave a pasty smile, "I will do what I can to protect her."

2 A TALL TALE

By six o'clock I had finished work for the day. Giles had left hours before and I was leaning back in my chair trying to decide what and where to eat when Donetta returned. She bounced up the stairs and started banging around in the kitchen in her usual lightning preparation of a meal. I went in and gave her the message.

She flung the wooden spoon down into the saucepan of soup she was stirring and looked at me with irritation.

"Bloody hell! and you told him I lived here?"

"Isn't he a friend of yours?"

"Not. He works for the police in my country and he is bad news for me."

Suddenly she looked fragile and I put a protective arm around her.

"Don't worry, he can't do anything here. If he keeps bothering you, go to the police."

"No police!"

My arm slipped from her shoulders and I staggered back wondering how long it would take my ear to clear. She stared at me frowning, then it began to dawn on her that she may have been a little too emphatic.

"I am sorry, but you don't understand, these people are capable of anything. They can work through official channels and make things difficult, maybe even get me deported. I will try to explain, but it is complicated."

"Don't tell me, the less I know the better."

"No, I might need your help, I know I can trust you. First I must phone my friend Mia at the Embassy to find out if she knows anything about Ivan."

I made some coffee and poured out two brandies to go with it while the sounds of a voluble and excited conversation floated down from the front room. I lit a cigarette and sat down to wait.

Donetta came back into the room frowning. "Mia

knew he was in the country, but doesn't know why. I hope he hasn't found out."

This last sentence she said almost to herself, then she gave a matter-of-fact smile and sat down. I pushed her brandy and coffee towards her and said: "So what is going on?"

"You don't know Zagreb," she said, "much of it is still beautiful. The main city, which was at one time two towns, runs from the Sava river to the Zagrebacka Gora. I lived in the low part near the student area, but what I have to tell you concerns Radic Square in Gric - that is what we call the high town.

"Radic Square is full of history. They say that Zagreb is the heart of Croatia and Radic Square is the heart of Zagreb. Nowadays, most of the buildings are government offices. The Parliament is there and also the Praesidium, which used to be the court of the Ban. Between these two stands St. Marks, on old Gothic church with brilliantly coloured tiles on the roof inscribed with the coats of arms of Croatia, Slovenia and Zagreb."

"Where does Ivan come in?" I asked, taking a sip of brandy.

"Wait, I'm trying to explain. Last year, before this

war began, I was working for Youth Radio in Zagreb. At that time the whole atmosphere was different. The old regime was changing and anything seemed possible. We did stories about Politics, Student Rights, Freedom and Art that would never have been allowed before. We had the courage to act on the new freedom and we believed we could make a difference.

"Anyway, a friend of mine called Jan, who also did some things for Youth Radio, came to see me one day with an idea. He is the son of one of the government ministers and he had got a summer job working in the vaults of the Sabor (the Parliament) sorting files. There is room after room of these cellars, which in fact are the cellars of the old Parliament house that had been built over when the new building had been put up in the 19th century.

"Jan was excited because it seems these cellars were only partly used. The ones housing files had electricity, but the rest didn't and were in complete disuse. He thought there might be forgotten artefacts, or old records left lying there for years and he wanted an excuse to investigate.

"I thought it would make a good story so I agreed to go with him. He told Gregoriavic, the clerk, that I was an archaeology student who was interested in the cellars and he asked if he could show me round after work. An alibi of research and study will get you most places and we got permission.

"The first few rooms consisted of metal racks filled with files and were as boring as the clerk who pointed them out to us. But we soon got past these and came to unlit, damp, lichen covered, stone vaulted rooms that had the right air of mystery and gloom.

"Jan went into raptures describing the old stonework and dating, completely spuriously, the crumbling pillars until Gregoriavic got fed up and left. He said he would carry on with his inventory for another half-hour, but he couldn't be too late or his wife would think he was out drinking.

"As soon as he had gone Jan waved his torch and led the way into the further chambers. These were in even worse repair, some stones had fallen from the ceiling and the walls were bulging and cracked. Finally, we came to a section that looked as though it had been only half built. Ancient rubble lay around in piles and the walls were rough hewn rock.

"Jan went over to a dark, broken down corner and started pushing stones aside. Following the light I bent down beside him.

'What are you doing?' I asked.

'I found this a few days ago - look.'

"Where he had been pulling at the stones there was a small gap. He shone the torch through. We could see what looked like a tunnel.

'Come on' he said.

"I began to feel nervous.

"We crawled through and stood up. We were obviously in some sort of connecting passage. The air was so damp and close I could hardly breathe. Eventually, we came to a door. Jan pushed and it opened. We stumbled down some steps and Jan shone the torch around.

"We were in another stone chamber. Coffins lined the walls, some were open and the bones had fallen or been taken out. Skulls gaped at us from dark corners. I moved closer to Jan and held his arm.

'What's this?' I whispered.

'It's got to be a crypt, we must be under St. Mark's.'

"Jan's jerkily moving torch suddenly came to rest on an object in the centre of the room. It was a sarcophagus, obviously belonging to a once important figure. He walked over to it, leaving me to stumble after him. The top was etched with Cyrillic writing. It was cold, stark, ominous. I leant over to try and read the inscription and my foot knocked against something. I told Jan to shine the torch.

"It was a leather briefcase and, to my horror, I saw that it was new.

'Who could have left this here?' I wondered.

'Let's find out' answered Jan, as he flicked the catches."

Donetta's hand reached slowly forward and touched me on the arm. Her wide open jade eyes were regarding me with the look of a startled cat.

"There are some evil people in the world, Peter" she said, quietly.

I paused long enough to appear to give due weight to the remark and then said: "What was in it?"

"A silver dagger with a grotesque devil figure as the handle, a silver bowl, an old missal and a black silk cloth with a burning crown embroidered on it in gold. Jan and I looked at each other."

'Occult rites, maybe black mass' he whispered.

"For a moment there was no sound but our breathing. We stood like stone statues in the mouldering darkness surrounded by the silent dead.

Suddenly, the torch went out and there was a maniacal, ghostly laugh. Two arms clasped me from behind. My insides gave a convulsive leap, as if I had received an electric shock and I let out a terrified scream.

'Shh! for Christ's sake, you'll wake the dead.'

"It was Jan with his arm around me staring anxiously into my face.

'I was only trying to be funny to make us see how stupid all this is.'

"I looked at him as if he was one step lower than a slug. I could have kicked him.

'Come on' Jan said, 'We had better get back, or old Gregoriavic will come looking for us.'

"He took my hand and, shining the torch, led the way out. I was too stunned by the whole unreal scene and Jan's joke to do anything more than follow dumbly until we got back to the main cellars and could once more see each other under electric light.

"Gregoriavic was violently pulling files from the shelves throwing them on the floor and muttering to himself as we came in.

'Ah!' he said, 'so you decide to return. You have been away forty five minutes. Not only do I have to fetch the files myself, but my wife is at this moment pouring my last bottle of plum brandy down the sink, thinking I am going to come home drunk.'

"He looked at me.

'What's wrong young lady, you look as if you had seen a ghost?'

"I tried to laugh. 'It is the air in these cellars, it's like walking in a tomb.'

"Gregoriavic grunted: 'And did you see anything that would help you in your studies?'

'Nothing but crumbling stone and spiders' laughed Jan, 'I think Donetta expected to find the sword of King Bela, at the very least.'

"He looked at me, hunched up, hands in my pockets beside him.

'You're cold, we will go to a cafe and have a chocolate to warm up.'

"He turned to Gregoriavic. 'Thank you for waiting, it seems I owe you a bottle of plum brandy.'

"Gregoriavic shrugged, but his eyes took on a roguish gleam. I could see that what I had taken to be a complaint had in fact been a subtle hint. We left on the best of terms.

"It wasn't until we got into the warmth of the cafe that I began to recover and an idea for a story began to form in my mind. I knew we could not openly discuss what we had found, but I thought we could get St. Mark's to let us do a programme on the history of the church with reference to the rise of the new Croatia. We might even get into the crypt. Then, if we found any evidence of secret meetings, we would be in the company of priests and other people, so we wouldn't be implicated.

"I told Jan and he became excited about the idea. Some friends joined us and we described what we had seen. We made it terrifying - skeleton hands dangling from coffins, bats fluttering, the sound of ghostly plainsong echoing from above. We were proud of ourselves.

"Suddenly, Jan, with a wink at me, rummaged in his bag and pulled out a leather bound, flimsy paged book and banged it on the table. It was the missal from the briefcase.

'Oh Jan, I am cross with you' I said, 'you shouldn't have!'

'Why not?' he cried, 'I don't like their little games. Maybe it is their turn for a shock, maybe they will think one of the dead monks took it.'

"He flicked the pages, markings and annotations were scattered throughout the text, but when he got to the flyleaf he stopped.

'Hey!' he exclaimed, 'what's this?'

"A list of names in black Gothic script ran down the page. He leant forward and began to read: 'Tomckin, Fonescu, Dimitric...'

"He looked up. Our faces were pale. These were the names of some of the top people in government. There was a moment's silence, then everybody started talking at once. Absent mindedly, I was fidgeting with the buttons on my dress. Suddenly, they all stopped and looked at me.

'Donetta, what's wrong?'

"I was sitting frozen, I must have looked sick.

'It's my silver name brooch' I said, 'I've lost it.'

She paused and lit a cigarette.

"Did you lose it in the tomb?" I asked.

"The crypt. I don't know - probably - maybe when Jan played his joke."

"What did you do?"

"I got scared and went to my uncle and told him the whole story. I was planning to come to England anyway and he agreed to help me. Before I left I phoned Jan and told him what I was doing. He said that it was a good idea and that he was going to lie low for a while himself. I thought it was all over, but now maybe they are trying to contact me through

Ivan. These people are not to be trusted - I must be very careful."

This story was so bizarre I almost believed it. In my mind's eye I saw a shadowy group of paunchy middle aged figures, gathered in a darkened crypt, performing sinister occult rites to bind them irrevocably together. A conspiracy at the highest level - but for what? And why hadn't she heard from Jan?

I watched her pouring another brandy, an expression halfway between amusement and self satisfaction playing about her eyes. Anyone less like a tragic pawn in a political game would have been hard to imagine.

"The whole thing seems weird" I said, "but you may be blowing it out of proportion. It is unlikely that they would have been able to trace who had been in the crypt even if they found the brooch and, if they had, what would they gain by sending Ivan after you?"

Her eyes flashed angrily.

"Well I don't know, do I? But Jan is still there and he would say or do anything if he thought he could create a bit of excitement. He has very strong ideas, most of them against the status quo, old or new.

There has got to be some reason why a secret service man who is also a member of the Ustase is over here."

"Come on, you're making this up. This is 1993 the Ustase died out at the end of the war."

"Huh! Those sorts of organisations are like vampires, a little new blood and they come back to life."

"All right, have it your own way. You are a dangerous subversive and they have sent Ivan to eliminate you. What do you want me to do?"

"Nothing - I can see you think I'm crazy. It is not your problem, so you can forget the whole thing. I should never have told you. Anyway, I can look after myself."

She flicked her head defiantly and stubbed her cigarette out in the ashtray as if I were under it.

3 THE BURGLARY

A blustery wind was ruffling the leaves at the edge of the common as I turned down by the Pavement and back towards the flat. People still lingered outside the Prince of Wales pub, drunkenly talking, and a would-be passenger stood at a bus stop hunched against the wind.

I had been checking out a few venues and had had a whisky or two in each one, so as I let myself in I only vaguely wondered why the catch on the Yale lock was so loose.

I went into the kitchen/dining area, flicked on the light switch and had got as far as picking up the kettle from the cooker before I sensed that something was wrong. I glanced round. The room was in turmoil. Cupboards were open, drawers had been pulled out and emptied on the floor. Chairs were overturned.

Slowly, I put down the kettle and went up to the front room. It was as bad, my files had been pulled out, the desk had been rifled, the sofa moved. It looked as if half a dozen children had been using the place as an adventure playground for a week. I consoled myself by thinking that poverty had prevented the loss of anything valuable.

I was about to phone the police when a thought struck me. Was Donetta at home? I went along to her room and knocked on the door. No answer. I gently opened it and looked in.

Another disaster area. I never would have believed she had this many clothes. It made me feel that every charity shop between Clapham and Portobello must be standing empty. I pushed the door open wider and went in.

A tube of toothpaste had been squeezed out over the futon. A box of compact powder had been emptied. Even a terra-cotta bedside lamp had been smashed - somebody was looking for something.

Over against the wall, on the far side of the futon was a pile of clothes. I looked at it apprehensively.

Was it big enough to conceal Donetta's five foot one inch frame? I forced myself to reach a shrinking hand towards it. Suddenly the deafening sound of a fire bell rang in my ear. I sprang back, knocking against the wall. It rang again. I pulled aside a towel and picked up the phone.

"Hello."

"Oh Peter, thank God it's you." The voice was small and strained.

"Donetta! Where are you?"

"It doesn't matter now - listen, you're in danger."

"Me!"

"Yes, you must leave immediately - and don't forget, bring your leather jacket."

I took a deep breath and tried to speak with the voice of quiet reason.

"Firstly, why am I in danger? Secondly, are you aware that the flat has been burgled? And thirdly, it is almost certainly your fault."

A few impatient and dismissive clicks came over the phone, as if to say 'We've no time for this silliness now'. Then she said: "Listen, get out as fast as you can. I will leave a message for you at the Noire tomorrow. Don't forget the leather jacket, I have sewn my ring into the lining."

"What!" I no longer sounded like the voice of quiet reason. "This is my home. I'm not leaving because some hooligan is after you, probably with justification. I'm going to the police."

"Don't!" There was panic in her voice. Please, just wait for a day until I can explain. I am sorry, I must go now, good-bye." She hung up and I was left listening to the dial tone.

I stood still for a moment, then slammed down the receiver. I went into my room and found my leather jacket. There was a lump at the bottom of the lining. What was the stupid bitch playing at?

Four hard knocks rocked the front door. The wrecked flat and the phone call had had their effect. I froze, cursing himself for not having turned the key in the mortice lock. The Yale would give at a push. There was another knock on the door. It acted like an electric shock. I grabbed the jacket and slipped quietly down the back stairs into the garden. Behind me the front door clicked open.

The maisonette was in a row of connecting houses, so the quickest way out to the street was through the ground floor flat. My downstairs neighbour was Mrs Knowles, a thickset, heavy jowled old woman who was virtually an invalid. She lived alone with a fat, overbearing cat. I hoped I wouldn't frighten her, I was frightened enough for the two of us.

Climbing the rickety fence I sneaked up to the back door and tapped on it quietly. Nothing. This was no time for standing on ceremony. I tried the handle. The door opened and I went through a small back door area int the kitchen.

Mrs Knowles was reclining in an armchair, her swollen legs up on a stool, in front of a gas cooker with the oven door open to keep her warm. The cat was under the sideboard. A stale smell mixed with the smell of cat food pervaded the room.

As I came into the room she sat forward and, in a fear laden but stentorian voice, yelled: "What do you want?"

"Shhh" I said, pointing upwards and holding a finger to my lips. "It's Pete, Mrs. Knowles - remember? There are burglars upstairs. I managed to get out the back way without them seeing me."

"Mrs. Knowles calmed down.

You're the man who lives upstairs aren't you?"

Although she had lowered her voice considerably it still reverberated like a lorry in low gear. I smiled reassuringly, then shut the door and bolted it.

"I almost phoned the police earlier" she said, "I heard a lot of bumps and bangs. It sounded as if there was a fight going on."

"It's the same people" I said, "they have come back."

"That's odd" she said, pensively, then she snapped into action. "Quick, there's the phone, ring the police."

I hesitated. I didn't want to ignore Donetta's plea without finding out her reasons, on the other hand, I couldn't walk out on a frightened old woman who might think she was in danger. I looked at Mrs. Knowles heavy, wispy haired chin and met her penetrating gaze - I picked up the receiver.

"Clapham police station."

"Hello, I want to report a break-in at 34 Bromells Road."

"Yes, we know." The voice was patiently professional. "It has been reported, there is a car on the way."

I thanked him and put down the phone.

"Well?" said Mrs. Knowles.

"Somebody has already told them, they are sending a car."

"I expect they were seen going in" said Mrs.

Knowles, with satisfaction, "you had better wait outside, then you can give a description if they try to leave before the police arrive."

I went down the passage, eased open the door and stood in the shadows. A few moments later a small, Ford Escort patrol car drew up. Two policemen got out and came towards me.

"I think they are still in there" I said.

I opened the door and followed them upstairs. The flat felt deserted, there was no sound of movement. Then I heard a voice coming from the front room.

"Is that you Pete?" It was a light attractive voice, but nervous. I recognised it.

"Claire! Are you all right?"

Footsteps rushed to the landing.

"Pete, you've been burgled. I phoned the pol..."

She stopped as she looked over the banister.

"Oh, you're here."

"I'm Sergeant Michael and this is Constable Collins. Was it you who phoned?" The policeman who had spoken was now at the top of the stairs. He was about six foot three and weighed a good sixteen stone. I thought he must be a contortionist in his spare time, otherwise he would never have squeezed into the patrol car.

Claire turned and led the way into the front room.

"Yes I got here ten minutes ago. I live just around the corner. I do some secretarial work for Pete and came to drop off some contracts." She glanced at me. "You said you would be back by eleven."

"I'm sorry, it slipped my mind." I decided not to mention my earlier tactical retreat.

"Anyway" Claire continued, "I knocked a couple of times and then the door more or less fell open. I came in to wait, saw the mess and phoned you."

Sergeant Michael nodded while eyeing the mess casually, too casually I thought. He asked Constable Collins to check the other rooms. It took him about thirty seconds and he wasn't moving quickly. As he sighed his way back into the front room, the two exchanged knowing glances. They seemed not just unimpressed, but disinterested. If I had not wanted to keep their involvement to a minimum, I would have been annoyed.

"Have you noticed anything missing?" Sergeant Michael was looking at me accusingly.

"No, but I haven't checked yet."

"No cash, jewellery, or other valuables?" Constable Collins felt he had me on the run and was keeping up the pressure.

"I don't know, there was not much here."

"Lucky - we will send Forensic round in the morning to dust for prints, don't touch anything until he has been. Afterwards, make a list of missing items and drop it into the station. Any problems, don't hesitate to get in touch."

I assured them I would and they left. I turned to Claire.

"Brandy?"

"Tea, please."

We picked our way through the chaos to the kitchen and I put on the kettle. Claire removed some rifled papers from a chair and sat down. She did not have Donetta's hourglass figure, but she had a slim, self contained beauty that, with her impish face and carefully disarranged dark brown hair, gave her the look of a fashion conscious waif. She started pushing an ashtray around the table with one finger.

"Where did you leave the contracts?" I asked.

"On your desk."

The kettle boiled. I threw a tea bag into a mug and poured in the water.

"Peter?"

I threw the tea bag out and added milk.

"What?"

"What actually did happen?"

I handed her the tea and poured myself a brandy.

"I've been burgled that's all, but it's no big deal, they can't have taken much."

"How do you know? You weren't bothered when you came in with the police and you haven't checked anything - and whose are all these clothes?"

"Donetta's, she is a waitress at the Noire who needs a place to stay for a couple of months. Giles recommended her and I need the rent."

"Well she is not going to be too pleased about this is she?"

"It's all right, she already knows..." I looked up. Claire was regarding me quizzically.

"Just a burglary?"

"Yes" I snapped, "just a burglary. Donetta asked me not to tell the police until she had had time to explain. She told me to take the ring in the jacket and leave in case they came back.

"What ring, and who are they?"

"All right, I'll tell you. It is all perfectly simple and nothing to do with me anyway."

I told her what I knew while Claire sat and looked superior.

"Hmm," she said, dryly, when I had finished, "let's have a look at it."

I was about to rip the lining of my jacket when I remembered Donetta's warning. The smashed terra-cotta lamp and squeezed toothpaste came into my mind.

"No, we had better get out of here. You can look at it later. I'll walk you home."

4 CLAIRE

Claire worked for a film animation company and that fact was reflected in the up to the minute retro decoration of her flat. There were plants, polished wood floors and open fires, with walls of that smoky red colour you usually only see in Sunday magazine articles. Odd little models and figurines crowded the mantelpiece, materials draped the chairs and small boxes of stones, beads and wires, which she used for making jewellery in her spare time, cluttered the top of the chest of drawers. A computer screen saver rolled in garish colours from the corner of the room.

Amid the smell of Jasmine tea and joss sticks, she examined the ring under an angle poise lamp.

"I would say it is a very good quality antique" she

said, finally, breaking the dismal sound of the rain outside, "probably at least eighteen carat gold, with a flawless dark red ruby, and, if the design is anything to go by, Fifteenth or Sixteenth century Mid-European. But look at these letters stamped on the inside - A.E.I.O.U. I wonder what they stand for?"

"A maker's mark?" I suggested.

"I don't think so, but if you want me to find out I have a friend who deals in antique jewellery."

"I had better ask Donetta first because, if my guess is correct, there may be more than one opinion as to who owns it."

She raised a delicate eyebrow as she handed it back to me. I pretended not to notice.

"Where are you going to stay tonight?" she asked, "it might make things easier if you did not go back to the flat until the police have dusted for prints. You're welcome to the couch."

I couldn't see that working although I appreciated her asking. It was too late to change things now.

"No thanks. I have to see Isaac - he has some publicity for me."

Even though it was well past midnight the Edgeware Road was humming and the Middle Eastern cafes and the take-aways were still open. I hadn't eaten since lunch time and I instinctively knew there would be slim pickings at Isaac's, so I called into a cafe and had a chicken shawarma and a coffee. Isaac would be out gigging and would not be in until late anyway.

I was still thinking about Claire. The whole thing had been my fault. Giving up a lack lustre music career and starting the agency had been harder than I had expected. Even though the independence of the agency was a good second option, I still hadn't liked the change and I had taken my anger and frustration out on her. I had more or less deliberately destroyed our relationship. She had eventually got fed up with what she called my self destructive attitude and had broken off the engagement. I thought she was right, she had spent enough time propping up a loser. The surprising thing was she had insisted on still helping with the business. I looked at my watch - 12.50. a.m. - I decided to give it another ten minutes.

I phoned Isaac at one o'clock. There was no surprise in the voice that told me to come round. It was still raining when I left the phone box.

Isaac lived on the first floor of a disused eighteenth century house in Daventry Street which is about halfway between Marylebone Station and the Edgeware Road. He opened the door and I followed him into darkness. Bits of old wood and furniture were stacked in the hall, aggressively invisible in the gloom. Uncarpeted stairs led up to a flat which consisted of two rooms knocked into one and a walk-in kitchen. Isaac put on the kettle.

He was a big, awkwardly built man with a tousled head of curly black hair over a dark eyed humorous face, which, when he was not talking, he held slantingly downwards, his mouth in a half grin, half grimace, as if he was enjoying some private joke that was causing him pain.

The room was a clutter of musical instruments, music books and manuscript. An acoustic guitar and a mandolin hung on the wall over a keyboard and two cases containing a soprano and an alto sax stood in the middle of the floor where they had obviously been dumped after that night's gig.

While waiting for the kettle to boil, he wandered nervously round the room. Pulling a trumpet from beneath some blankets he started to play haltingly, explaining between phrases that he had picked it up in a junk shop. The kettle boiled and, as he made tea, he kept up a low drone from the kitchen on Arts

Council grants, no gigs and audiences being a load of Neanderthals. Re-emerging, he put two chipped mugs on the table and sat down.

"Been kicked out of your flat? You should move into a squat."

"I've been burgled and I have to leave everything as it is until the police can dust for prints. I decided that the easiest way was to stay somewhere else for the night and collect that publicity from you at the same time."

"Any idea who did it?"

I went through the story again and showed him the ring.

"It looks valuable. If there is a history to it, we could have something."

"We wouldn't have anything, it's Donetta's."

Isaac grinned cynically.

"Bourgeois morality raises its drivelling head. If this ring is genuine, people have killed for it before and now it's our turn. Property is theft These bastards think they can take what they like and the Devil take the hindmost. Well we're not so dumb. Possession is nine tenths of the law. That means it is ours and no one else has a right to it."

"I thought that, according to your philosophy,

everyone has a right to it."

"They do, if they can take it, but it is not so difficult to get guns - we can defend ourselves."

I laughed, this was typical Isaac.

"I'm serious" he continued, frowning and smiling at the same time as his mind played over the possibilities, "or else we could drop it in a glass of wine and dissolve it. I've got some here."

"I think you are talking about pearls not rubies, but if you have got a bottle of wine, we could find a use for it."

Isaac produced the wine and two grubby water glasses, then he began searching aimlessly for a bottle opener. Finally, he found one under a newspaper written in Arabic. As he picked up the opener, he pointed to the paper.

"I found it in the street, I thought they might be advertising for musicians to work in Saudi Arabia."

"I didn't know you could read Arabic."

"I can't" he replied, and started to open the wine like a man drilling for oil.

We drank in silence for a few moments, then he said:

"You had better stay here for a couple of days until you find out what Donetta is up to. If what she told you is true, then it is political, but more likely she stole the ring and God knows what else and they are after her for it. This guy might be from the cops, or he might not. Either way it is none of your business."

I helped myself to another glass of wine and stuck a cigarette in my mouth from a packet on the table.

"I don't know" I said, as I lit up, "She is obviously frightened, but I can't believe the ring is stolen. If it was, why show it to me?"

"She showed it to you before she knew Ivan was around - and as soon as she did know, she hid it. That sounds like guilt to me."

"I think there is more to it. She is an intelligent, artistic girl with liberal ideas. The way her country is at the moment she might easily get on the wrong side of one political faction or another, especially as she did some journalistic work out there."

"Don't tell me" said Isaac, "she's beautiful."

I felt myself redden. "That's a cheap shot and has nothing to do with it."

"Of course not, she just looked at you with her baby blue eyes and told you of the dark forces moving against poor, freedom loving, little her. She knows we're all suckers for stories of political oppression over here."

"Why not? It happens."

"Maybe, but not as often as people with baby blue..."

"Green."

"Sorry, green eyes tell lies."

"Interesting, as it is, to have the benefit of your profound knowledge of human nature, you are knocking yourself out unnecessarily, I am hardly involved."

"You might believe that, but I know you are a closet Don Quixote and therefore vulnerable."

"Bullshit. Now, where can I sleep?"

"The people downstairs are away. I have a key because I am supposed to be looking after the place. I know they won't mind if you stay there for a couple of days, especially if you water the plants. I haven't got round to it yet and they have been away a week."

I agreed and he led me down to the ground floor. The flat was the same size as Isaac's, but more work had been done on it. There were plants hanging from the ceiling, lodged in corners and lined along shelves. The two rooms had not been knocked into one, but there was no door between them. Instead a heavy Mexican blanket on large wooden rings hung across the doorway. Both rooms were clean and comfortable and furnished with unmatched pieces of solid wooden furniture. The whole decor told you that the place belonged to people who were once alternative, but were now doing well in some profession.

Isaac showed me round and, after pointing a meaningful finger at the watering can, left. A little while later I heard the mournful sound of a clarinet drifting down from above.

5 THE RING

Martins from Forensic was small, quiet and meticulous. For two hours he picked his way through the mess dusting for prints, while I leant against doorways and watched. While working on the last room, he casually asked me if I was insured.

"No" I replied, "there is hardly anything here worth insuring."

Martins looked up momentarily and then carried on working.

"This job wasn't done by professionals" he said, "too much unnecessary mess."

"Probably kids" I said, the bastard probably thought I had burgled the place myself.

"Lucky for them to pick a house with an easy

lock."

"And unlucky for them" I continued, "to pick one where there was so little to steal."

"No doubt - well that about wraps it up. You can put the place back together again now. When you find out what is missing, drop a list round to the police station."

After he had gone I threw everything unceremoniously back in to cupboards, on to shelves and in to rubbish bags, then I made some coffee and settled down to work.

Martins' dull professionalism had made the events of the night before seem remote. I no longer felt the threat of danger. It was surely Donetta's sense of drama getting the better of her. I would tell the police nothing was missing and the incident would be closed. If it was Ivan who had broken in and if he had been after the ring, it was almost certainly a family matter and I had no business getting involved. The next step was to give the damn thing back to her.

I phoned the Noire, but no one had seen her. I told them where I would be and said I would call back later. By this time it was two o'clock, I had finished any work that needed immediate attention and I was ready to leave.   I thought I had better see if Mrs. Knowles was all right before calling in at the police station on my way back to Isaac's.

She let me in and ponderously led the way in to the kitchen, asking if the police had had any luck so far.

"No" I said, "and I doubt they will, but it doesn't matter as nothing of value seems to be missing.

The cat was lying by the open oven door, the curtains were drawn and a dim light bathed the plastic checkered tablecloth in a warm yellow glow. Mrs. knowles lowered herself painfully back in to her chair and regarded me with a baleful eye.

"No one is safe these days" she boomed, "even reading the local newspaper is enough to give you nightmares. I think the only reason they print it is to scare old people into staying indoors. Not that you're safe then because half the time they will break in whether you're there or not."

I nodded. The cat wandered over and looked into the food bowl.

"Mind you, I'm not defenceless, this was my husband's." She reached down by her chair and picked up an evil looking knobkerrie.

"The first burglar to come through the window

gets this over the head. I've had plenty of practice beating carpets, I can tell you."

"There is nothing to worry about Mrs. Knowles. That burglar won't be back now he knows there is nothing to take and he certainly won't try to break in here."

"What makes you think that" she said, sharply.

"Well..." I tried to think of a convincing reason that wasn't the real one. "Your flat is too close. No one would be crazy enough to do a thing like that."

"Huh!" she snorted, tapping the knobkerrie against the side of the chair. Then she realised I was trying to be reassuring and came within a cat's whisker of smiling.

"Still, I was pleased to know you were up there last night, even if you were moving about at three o'clock in the morning."

My face, I hope, remained dead pan. I did not want her to see that her words had hit me like a kick in the stomach.

"I'm sorry, I couldn't sleep, I hope I didn't keep you awake too long."

"With my aches and pains the night hours are more like a vigil than a rest. Unless it becomes intrusive, it doesn't bother me."

She suddenly seemed to notice for the first time that I was standing and waved me to a chair.

"Thank you," I said, "but I had better go, I've got a few things to do."

She didn't appear to be too disappointed and I let myself out.

The street was almost deserted. A man was working on a car, a mother and child were meandering slowly along and a postman was delivering letters. Nobody looked suspicious. I walked quickly away towards the police station.

The desk sergeant was reserved until he found out there was nothing to be done, then he became the epitome of cheerful professionalism.

"I am glad to hear that nothing was taken, sir. Nevertheless, we are working on it and if anything comes up, we will let you know." He smiled impersonally and turned to deal with an old couple who were complaining about noisy neighbours.

I caught the bus back to Marylebone. Isaac had been talking sense, it would be wise to stay out of the way while I still had the ring. After that it would be Donetta's problem. I let myself in to the vacant flat, threw myself into a chair and pulled the ring from my pocket.

So she had been right, the burglar had come back and this was the reason. I studied it closely. The dark red ruby and the intricate gold niello weaving like flames around it glinted in the afternoon sunlight. I imagined its history as it passed from hand to hand. Given as a gift, stolen as booty, inherited, spinning through time to land in a back street of Marylebone, once more to be argued over and fought for and once more to out live its possessor.

I was beginning to feel like an idiot. My home had been broken into, I was hiding out and I was looking after a piece of jewellery that was in all probability stolen - and all because a girl had asked me to. I felt my forehead, it seemed normal, although I would not have liked to have been seen by a psychiatrist.

I only had Donetta's word that it had been Ivan who had broken into the flat and, even if it had been him the first time, who had Mrs knowles heard at three o'clock in the morning? It wouldn't have been Ivan, so there was someone else involved. Maybe Donetta would know who it was. It might even convince her to go to the police.

I had a shower and went out to get something to eat at a nearby cafe before phoning the Noire. This time there was a message. Donetta would be in a Spanish bar in Hanway Street at eight thirty that evening.

I went back and called up to see Isaac who was making tea and eating an apple when he let me in. He looked as though he had been asleep for a week. I told him about the second person in the flat, but he only grunted and carried on with what he was doing. Eventually, he handed me a mug of tea.

"Ever heard of Mike Zollenhorn?" he asked.

"No."

"I met him at the Noire. He has a place down in Devon where he runs arty week-ends, mostly for charity. The main charity being Mike Zollenhorn. Me and Rico have been asked to do a free gig there this week-end."

"Speaking as your agent, I am unimpressed" I said. "How am I supposed to keep your price up if you're prepared to work for nothing?"

He didn't reply, he just handed me a leaflet. It was in black and white on glossy paper and folded concertina style. On the front was a picture of an old farmhouse set among trees. The caption read: 'Oakwood, The Natural Centre For Psychic Healing. Far from the ills and stresses of modern life, set deep in the heart of the rolling Devon countryside, the Oakwood Centre offers peace and regeneration.' There followed a list of the different performers and activities to be featured over the next two months. A few blues and jazz people from America, a classical quartet, an Indian dance troupe, a Croatian duo playing Cello and flute and Isaac's duo.

"Good photo of you" I lied, as I handed it back.

"I didn't show it to you to drum up a half hearted compliment. The whole thing is crap anyway. A bunch of phonies going round pretending how nice everything is while taking these bourgeois, imitation alternative types for everything they can get; but I was looking at it this morning and it reminded me that Zollenhorn is an expert on antique jewellery and paintings and stuff. He also knows places like Turkey, Bulgaria and Yugoslavia well, so he should be able to tell you about that ring."

"Thanks, I'll tell Donetta, but she thinks she knows all she needs to know - and Devon is a long way."

"He has a gallery near Bond Street and I wasn't thinking of Donetta, you should check it out before you give it back. At the moment, you don't know what you're getting into."

"I'm not getting into anything" I said, "after tonight, it won't be any of my business."

Isaac had picked up a saxophone and was fingering it silently. He moved over to the music stand.

"No problem then" he said.

6 KNOCKED OUT

Hanway Street is a narrow lane running between Tottenham Court Road and Oxford Street. I got there just before eight thirty. The Tarrega bar is squeezed between a second hand record shop and a Japanese restaurant. I pushed the door open and saw a dingy corridor. Straight ahead was a kitchen and to the right a cramped wooden staircase. I followed this down and found myself in a small oblong room with a bar, six or seven tables and a tiny stage. The walls were decorated with Spanish tourist ads and Flamenco posters.

Donetta was sitting hunched in her coat at a table in the corner. She saw me and waved. I sat down beside her and she silently poured me out a glass of house red.

"I thought you were supposed to be working at the Noire tonight?"

"I was but I told the girls to tell Leo I was ill. Ivan might go there."

"You were going to explain" I said.

She put her hand on my arm. "Oh I will" she said, "have you got the ring?"

I slipped it into her pocket and her eyes melted with gratitude.

"I don't forget people who help me" she said.

"That's good to know, but unless you can assure me there won't be anymore trouble, I will have to go to the police."

She pouted like a sulky child. "So you won't help me?"

"What more can I do? If Ivan intends to continue to break into flats, then he should be in jail. You have to face it. If it is your ring, you won't be thrown out of the country because you went to the police to prevent someone stealing it."

My voice had risen and I noticed with embarrassment that a group of austere Spaniards with loads of duende sitting a couple of tables away were looking at me. I reached for my cigarettes.

Donetta leaned forward with a smile.

"Shh, you don't have to tell the whole world. Now listen, I want your advice. The only way to get rid of Ivan is to pay him, he is just out for himself. I have a second ring which I believe is valuable." She held up her right hand, another ruby ring adorned the third finger. "Where can I find out what it is worth?"

"I've no idea" I said, surprised at this new angle, "I suppose you could take it to Hatten Garden."

"I knew you would know who to go to." She drew the ring from her finger and pressed it into my hand. "I am no good at business, I get too nervous. Will you take it for me - please?"

"I don't know enough about jewellery to accept an offer on your behalf. You will have to go yourself."

I tried to give the ring back, but she wouldn't take it.

"Peter, please" she whispered, don't make us conspicuous. I can't do it myself and I don't have anyone else in this country I can trust. You're the only one who can do this thing for me."

I glanced round, the Spaniards were still watching. I gave in and dropped the ring into my pocket. "Don't expect me to haggle" I said, "I'll just take the money and go."

She smiled a cat like smile. "You are a darling - have some more wine."

She said she could contact Ivan through the embassy and arrange to meet him somewhere crowded the next evening. She would tell him she had sold the ring, but that she still had most of the money. She would ask him to give it to her uncle for her. He would keep it of course, it was just a tactful way of bribing him. I was to meet her with whatever I had raised at six o'clock at the Noire and we would go along together.

"It won't work" I said, "but I'll do it if only because it will give me a chance to tell Ivan what I think of his burglary technique.

Donetta seemed to relax. "Don't worry" she said, "after tomorrow we will have no more problems."

The lights on Tottenham Court Road were garishly bright after the relative darkness of Hanway Street. The fish bar was doing good business and the Dominion Theatre's latest brash show faced across the road. I flipped up the collar of my leather jacket against the cold and started walking northward. I had agreed to get the ring valued more because I wanted to see what happened than anything else. I was becoming interested in Donetta's scatterbrained antics. There must be a logic to them somewhere, but at the moment nothing made sense.

I turned left at Howland Street towards Marylebone. There was a fine misty rain falling which added to the chill and made me walk faster. I called into an off-license and bought a half bottle of Martel, it would go well with the coffee when I got back to Isaac's.

I had reached a deserted Bell Street off Lisson Grove and had only a couple of hundred yards to go when something exploded against the side of my head. I staggered sideways and fell into a doorway thinking I had somehow or other walked into a lamp post. I rolled over and looked up. Two of the Spaniards were looming dark and solid against the night sky.

"Give me the ring."

They aren't Spanish, I thought, they're Italian."

I tried to sit up.

"What ri...?" A boot in the face cut short the word and my head snapped back and hit the door. A deft hand frisked me, then I heard a muttered 'Grazzi' and they were gone.

Slowly, I sat up and put a hand carefully to the side of my face. It felt painfully numb. I tried not to think of how damaged I might be, or how bad I was going to feel when the numbness wore off.

My head was splitting. After a moment or two I grabbed a railing and dragged myself to my feet. Thank God Isaac's is so close, I thought, and started off in a weaving aching stagger. It wasn't close enough, I passed out as I got to the front steps.

7 IVAN

A pale washed out face, two dark rimmed eyes and a mop of brown uncombed hair advanced and receded before me. I closed my eyes and concentrated on the buzzing in my head. No good. I only became more aware of the thumping in my ears that accompanied it. I opened my eyes again and the face came to a standstill. I knew that face from somewhere, maybe in a past life. Once more my head whirled dizzily, then things started to clear.

"What happened?"said Giles. "Me and Isaac found you on the doorstep. You're plenty heavy to carry."

"You got plastered, man, and fell over." Isaac's large curly head appeared round Giles' shoulder, smiling painfully. He handed me a cup of tea. It was hot and sweet.

"I was mugged" I said, thickly. The left side of my face felt like a football. I touched it and brushed against dried blood. Then I remembered the brandy, by some miracle it was still in one piece. I put it on the table while Isaac assembled the glasses. I soaked a handkerchief and held it against my cheek while pouring out three stiff ones, then I told them what had happened.

"Maybe these Italians saw Donetta give you the ring and decided to hit you for it" suggested Isaac.

"No, too much of a coincidence, but Donetta may not have known who they were."

"No way" said Giles, "she would never do a thing like that."

I glanced at him to catch a trace of sarcasm, but there was nothing. I carried on.

"Up until now" I said, "it has been simple. Donetta has this ring which she says is 'very special'. Where she got it we don't know. A couple of days ago this character called Ivan comes looking for her and she says he is dangerous, a member of a right wing group who is after her because she has discovered, as far as I can work out, nothing. Then the flat is broken into. What are they after? Not Donetta, but the ring. They don't get it because, naturally, she has sown it into my jacket. The next thing is I get mugged by two Italians. A clear sequence of events that obviously has a clear explanation, the question is, what is it?"

"I told you, go to Zollenhorn..."

"Zollenhorn!" exclaimed Giles.

Isaac ignored him and continued: "That ring may be as special as Donetta says it is and, if it is, he would know. But it's too late now, you've given it back. Pass the brandy."

I poured out three more drinks and, as Giles took his, he tried again.

"I saw Zollenhorn this evening at the Noire" he said, "he's got this place in Devon where he puts on music and stuff."

"Yeah, yeah" said Isaac, "we know."

"Glad to hear it" continued Giles, "then you won't be surprised to learn that he is bringing in two musicians from Eastern Europe. He wants someone to look after them and maybe set them up a few gigs." He turned to me. "I mentioned you and he said you sounded perfect." He shook his head sadly. "I thought the agent was supposed to get the musician gigs, not the other way around."

I dabbed the handkerchief against my cheek to show that this was a time for sympathy, not recriminations, but he didn't notice.

"He is a good guy to get in with" he continued, "some of the people on your books (me for instance) are just what he needs."

"Maybe I will go and see him" I said, "but I can't concentrate on anything until I get a good night's sleep and have seen Donetta."

"Take my word for it" said Giles, "that girl is all right. One look at her face will tell you..."

Isaac patted him on the shoulder soothingly.

"I'm sure you're right and at any other time we would be happy to join you in your fairy tale world, but it's time Pete hit the sack."

I agreed and left, not forgetting to take what remained of the brandy with me.

The unoccupied flat was about as welcoming as a city park on a drizzling Sunday afternoon, but at least it was quiet and I could be alone. I washed my face in cold water, finished the last of the brandy and collapsed into bed.

After a while I heard Giles stumble down the stairs in the dark and out the door. Isaac creaked across the floorboards above and a jazz record came on. A drip from the kitchen tap maintained a steady rhythm and I tried to match it to the throbbing in my cheek. Finally, I fell asleep.

I had no idea what time it was when I awoke, it was still dark. It felt like four in the morning. For a few moments I stared into a blackness you could almost touch, then I heard a shuffling sound. It stopped, there was silence, then it started again. The window in the front room was being prized open I began to roll slowly out of bed, trying to keep as quiet as possible. The idea was to get onto my feet, although beyond that I had no plan. It did not matter. I heard the heavy curtain over the doorway being pulled to one side and, simultaneously, a powerful torch shone in my face.

"If you make noise, I will knock you out." The voice sounded young and foreign. My head didn't feel like taking anymore punishment, so I relaxed back on my elbow and waited.

"We have met before" the voice continued, "my name is Ivan. I followed you when you returned to your house this morning."

I recalled the innocent looking street and gave

myself nil for observation.

"I am sorry I had to break into your flat. I am working for the Croatian government and I was looking for information which I did not think could be got in any other way."

I did not say anything.

"Leon Taveric, who is Donetta's uncle, was a member of Tito's Politburo. His job was to oversee the museums and art treasures. The former aristocracy could not keep their collections, so anything of value was confiscated, collated and distributed to museums or to the special houses used by government ministers. Many pieces of inestimable value passed through his hands. Not all of them found their way to their proper destinations.

"Donetta has a ring which she stole, or maybe it was given to her, which I must get back. I doubt she realises the threat she is under if she keeps it."

"Donetta does have a ring" I said, "but she says it belongs to her family. Actually, she gave it to me tonight and asked me to have it valued."

The torch wavered fractionally and moved closer.

"Unfortunately, some people in the bar saw us discussing it, followed me when I left, cracked me over the head and took it."

The voice became mildly concerned.

"You have been beaten up?"

"Of course I have, I don't always look like this."

"You went to the police?"

"No, there is not much they can do."

"Would you recognise them again?"

"Yes, they were about eight foot tall, weighed about fifteen stone a piece and spoke in Italian accents."

"They were Italian?" He almost barked the words. It obviously meant something to him, something he did not like.

"You know who they were then" I said.

The torch retreated a little.

"It is nothing to concern yourself with" he said flatly, "so far Donetta has been lucky, take my advice and stay out of it." He switched off the torch, ducked back through the curtain and was gone.

I got up, turned on the light and lit a cigarette. For a member of the Croatian diplomatic staff he seemed to have taken to breaking and entering like a natural. So now at least I was sure who the first burglar had been and if I had to guess, I would have said the second was one of the people who had mugged me earlier. Whoever it was, the next move was to speak to Donetta. If the ring was hers, she should go to the police, if not, I would try and persuade her to do something sensible for a change and give it back.

8 WASTED WARNING

I awoke again at six and had a bath and a shave. I hadn't slept well, so I had decided to walk over to Fulham to clear my head and have breakfast on the way. I looked in the mirror and saw a bruised cheek and a black eye. It could have been worse.

The street lamps were still on as I left the house. The air was damp and cold and traces of fog mixed with the darkness. I had plenty of time, so I crossed the Marylebone Road and walked over towards Soho. Rubbish bags were piled up at intervals and isolated lights shone from a few cafes and newsagents. There weren't many people around and those who were had that positive spring in their step which comes from early rising. Buses rumbled along

Oxford Street seemingly unable to disturb the homeless sleeping in doorways wrapped in sleeping bags and blankets.

I stopped at a cafe in Poland Street and ordered orange juice, bacon, eggs, toast and tea. Behind the counter a man was somnambulantly making sandwiches and rolls and piling them in the window. He licked a bit of mayonnaise off his finger and pulled another two slices of bread towards him. I looked at him with distaste, after my experience of the night before I was beginning to take a dim view of Italians. Then the waitress arrived with my breakfast. She looked as if she had just fallen off a Roman vase into a pair of jeans. I had to admit they had their good points too.

The Noire opened at ten and I got there at about five past. It was empty except for Donetta, noisily sweeping the floor, and Pascal, a tall, dark haired French girl who did the cooking.

"Oo la la, what happened to you?" Donetta flung down the broom and rushed over to me, gently touching the bruise and muttering tch, tch, tch.

"I was mugged - they got the ring."

She took it well, waving her hand dismissively while guiding me to a table.

"I will make us two coffees and you can tell me everything."

Sympathy is soothing. I sat down feeling comfortably sorry for myself. She brought the coffees over and slid into a chair, her wide eyes giving me every attention.

I told her the story. She didn't seem surprised to hear that my attackers had been the people at the next table in the bar.

"I thought there was something strange about them" She said, "but it doesn't matter, the ring was of little value."

That would seem to prove that it had been a set up. I watched her take a sip of coffee before I said: "I have also seen Ivan."

She stared at me evenly, one raised eyebrow creasing a smooth forehead.

"He followed me to where I was staying and broke into my room in the early hours of the morning. We had a chat."

"Really?" She lit a cigarette and flicked her head back, blowing a thin stream of smoke into the air. "That seems unusually gentle for him. What did he say?"

"He told me the ring does not belong to your

family, it is the property of the government."

Her lip curled.

"They talk about a new democracy, but the same jackals are tearing at the carcass. The state does not own this ring, they have no right to it and never did have. Anyway, what is one ring more or less to a national treasury?"

"Listen" I said, "if there is one thing I learned from Ivan it is that you are out of your depth. Take my advice and give it back." But she was not listening. She was staring into space, the little brain clicking away like the well oiled machine it was.

"So, who does he think has it now?" she asked, suddenly.

"I told him the Italians have it."

She looked at me in surprise for a second, then she gave a light musical laugh.

"Two with one blow" she cried, "that is perfect."

I finished my coffee and stood up.

"If you won't take my advice there is nothing more I can do, but if you think you have heard the last of Ivan or the Italians you couldn't be more wrong."

I waved to Pascal and started for the door. Donetta grabbed my arm.

"Peter, wait!"

"When you need someone to get beaten up, or hold on to stolen goods for you, let me know, otherwise you're on your own."

As I went out the door I heard her say: "Thanks for protecting me Peter."

"Yeah, Yeah" I thought.

9 ZOLLENHORN

A Persian rug was draped in the centre of the window display, flanked by two delicate, highly polished, antique side tables with vases on them. That was it, nothing gaudy, nothing eye catching, all it said was, exclusive and expensive. Over the window in gold etched in marble were the words 'Zollenhorn. New York - Paris - London'.

Inside a fair haired debutante type, who'd been younger, was talking on the phone.

"Hello darling, would you mind awfully if we postponed tonight. It's just that George is coming up from Gloucestershire and he has promised to wine and dine me." Pause. "No I am not going to get involved again, that would be too boring. He suggested we try the Ritz where he is staying and it's yonks since I have been there." Pause, and then coldly "I think they have changed the chef since then." Another pause followed by a tinkling laugh. "I assume he is on expenses. Thanks darling, you're a sweetie. I'll phone you tomorrow."

A little sound effect kiss and the conversation was over. Replacing the receiver, she flicked her hair and gave me a smile that would have frozen a Paris mob.

"Can I help you?"

"Peter Delaney, to see Mr. Zollenhorn."

I will see if he is available." She reached languidly across the desk and picked up the phone. "Mr. Zollenhorn, I have a Mr. Delaney in reception." The reaction was obviously stronger than she had expected because one eyebrow moved a hair's breadth. She looked up.

"Would you like to go in?"

She pointed to a door that was flush with the wall and decorated in the same way, except for a glass handle just above the dado rail. I went in.

Zollenhorn was coming round the desk to meet me. He was thick set, about forty, five foot nine or ten, with the heavy face of a man who liked a good meal. He had full eyebrows and luxuriant black hair swept back and curling at the collar. He looked like a city banker.

"Pete, I don't think we've met. I'm Mike, thank you for taking the trouble to drop in. Sit down."

Shaking my hand, he guided me to a Louis XIV chair in front of the desk and resumed his seat.

"You are an agent who books a lot of European acts I believe."

"Well, I don't know about a lot, I..."

"As you may know" Zollenhorn swept on, "I am interested in the arts. I have this little place in Devon which I like to see as a sort of centre. Too often in our lives the emphasis is placed on the wrong things. 'The world is too much with us; late and soon, getting and spending we waste our powers', as Wordsworth would say. Down at Oakwood we like to create an environment that contributes to well being and inner peace on a personal level and also, in some small way, to the world at large."

I didn't say anything. He carried on.

"I am having an 'Arts for Peace' weekend in a few days time and I need someone to co-ordinate the acts coming in from Europe. Normally my secretary down there does it, but she is ill. I asked around and your name came up. Can you do it?"

"I should think so - what does it entail?"

"The main focus for the event is a Croatian duo from Zagreb called 'The new Day Ensemble'. They are wonderfully courageous people who are doing tremendous things out there. They are coming to Oakwood to try and awaken the conscience of the West."

"Will the conscience of the West be there?"

"Pardon?"

"Nothing, I was just wondering how many people you were expecting?"

"We can cater for about thirty in the house and cottages and maybe another twenty or so day guests. We don't aim for large crowds, we aim for special ones." He dismissed the subject with a slight wave of his hand and continued: "'The New Day Ensemble' are arriving in Paris in two days time. I want you to meet them, look after the arrangements and bring them to Oakwood. This is their first time in Western Europe and I don't want any hitches or confusion when they come into the country. I know this is more of a service than you are usually required to provide as an agent, but I need a man who is used to dealing with musicians. You would get expenses and £100 a day."

"What about visas and work permits?"

"That has been done."

"I can't see any problems then."

"Good." He handed me a computer print out. "Here are the details. They arrive at Gare Saint-Lazare on Thursday at 1500 hours and their first performance in Oakwood is on Friday evening. Here is a publicity photo to help you recognise them. Get a receipt for everything and we will sort it out when you get to Oakwood."

He stood up and stuck out his hand.

"Well, I won't keep you any longer, you have been a great help."

We shook hands and I went out past the secretary, who was listlessly leafing through Harpers or Vogue, or some equally riveting piece of nonsense.

10 NIGHT TRAIN TO PARIS

This job, although unusual, was more in my line and I was glad to get back to work after the distractions of the last couple of days. What I had to do was simple, so simple as to be almost unnecessary, but then some musicians need a lot of help and, if they are worth enough money to somebody, they get it.

I went back to the flat and wandered from the kitchen to the front room and back again. Although everything was back to normal, it felt strange. I checked the phone, no messages. Financially, this Zollenhorn job could be a life saver, especially if I was able to string it out over the week-end. I made myself some coffee and sat down to work. I had a few things to sort out before leaving for Paris on the night train the next day.

The pile of papers had done the circuit of the desk twice without diminishing noticeably when Claire phoned.

"I have been doing some research on that ring you showed me and I have found out the significance of those letters. If the ring is genuine, they mean it belonged to Frederick III of Austria, he had all his possessions stamped with them, including his wife for all I know."

"Interesting" I said, "because I found out from Ivan that she probably got it from her uncle who is something to do with redistribution of art treasures over there. He may have given it to her or she may have stolen it."

"Who is Ivan?"

"Some guy who works for the Croatian government and who is over here to try and get it back. There are some other people after it as well."

"Pete, do you know what you are getting into?"

"Don't worry, I'm not involved anymore. If she is smart she will either give it back to Ivan, or go to the police. I have to go to Paris tomorrow to nursemaid a couple of musicians down to a concert in Devon. I will give you a ring when I get back and tell you the whole story, maybe you will be able to make more sense of it than I can."

"I don't doubt that" she said, "but then maybe I'm not so susceptible to beautiful women with sad stories."

We said good-bye and I jerked another contract from the pile. She did not seem to like Donetta for some reason. I couldn't work out why - she had never even seen her.

By six o'clock I had finished. I put on a Bartok quartet, stretched myself out on the sofa and closed my eyes to concentrate. Half an hour later I was woken by the sound of the doorbell. I lowered the music and went to see who it was. The figure confronting me was tall, dark, carrying a briefcase and all too familiar.

"Mr. Delaney - we have met before, remember?"

He pushed me effortlessly aside and calmly strode upstairs to the flat. I remembered all right. My face still felt sore from his boot.

I followed him up and stood just inside the door. He was sitting by the fire, leaning back, relaxed.

"Donetta Taveric lives with you?"

"She rents a room here - that is she used to, I don't know where she is now. Who are you?"

"Luigi" he said with a smile, the wide comforting smile of a liar.

"Cigarette?" I decided to take the initiative in the hope of getting the chance to break something heavy over the back of his head.

He nodded and I threw one over while moving round the room as if searching for a lighter. My eye fell on a small brass figurine of Venus that I kept on the desk and I leaned casually towards it.

"Catch." I turned round and a lighter hit me in the chest. I caught it and lit up.

"Don't even think about it - unless you like hospitals" he said. "But I didn't come here to fight" he continued, "I came to apologise. We acted hastily." He opened the briefcase took out a bottle of Islay malt and placed it on the low table in front of him. "Get some glasses."

I dug out a couple of whisky glasses and, sitting down opposite him, put them beside the bottle. Solemnly, he uncorked it and poured out two large ones. We drank.

We put the glasses down. He looked me in the eye, I held his gaze. He poured two more. After the third one he slowed down enough to offer me a Gaulois. We lit up.

Suddenly, he reached into his jacket and threw the ring he had taken from me onto the table. I picked it up, studied it for a second and then pushed it into the pocket of my jeans.

"Donetta will be glad to get this back," I murmured.

"Delaney" he said, "Women are sometimes a little crazy" He tapped his forehead. "You and I, we know these things. Therefore, it is left to us to prevent more killing."

More killing! I didn't know there had been any. Who was this character? I had assumed he was some kind of criminal, but for all I knew he might have been an Italian shoe importer with a flare for 'in your face' promotion. I kept my face blank and leaned over to pour two more whiskies.

"Wanna tell me about it?" I said, I was beginning to feel like Humphrey Bogart.

"I want that ring" he said. "Its value is not important. It is a matter of family honour."

"That is Donetta's ring" I said, nodding at the one on the table. He ignored me and carried on.

"I come from Trieste. In the sixteenth century there was a marriage alliance between my family and the Habsburg's and part of the dowry was the ring. It had belonged to Frederick III and over the years it has been used more than once as a proof of allegiance to save the estate from the ravages of warring imperial troops. After the first world war we lost our estates, but my family managed to save some pieces of jewellery, among them this ring.

"As you know, the Italians and Germans invaded Yugoslavia in 1941 and my father took the ring with him when he was sent to Split on the Dalmatian coast. It was easy to carry and valuable and could be converted into hard cash if things turned out badly, which they did.

"He told me that when the partisans retook the city in 1943 he got separated from his unit and was left behind. His only hope was to make his way across country and see if he could get a fishing boat to take him to Italy. My father never went into details, but he had a hard time of it for a few days. Finally he fell in with a group of Chetniks who were going to Havr where some of their compatriots were still holding out. But the night before they were due to steal a fishing boat and make their way across to the island, my father was shot and robbed and left for dead in a deserted farmhouse. Their leader had changed his mind and had decided that his band's best chance was to join Tito's partisans.

"By some miracle, he was discovered the next day by two children whose father happened to be the local doctor. This man took him into his house, extracted the bullets and nursed him back to health. A couple of months later he persuaded the Germans to invalid him back to Italy."

Luigi paused and lit up another Gaulois. I took the opportunity to refill the whisky glasses. Eventually, he continued.

"At first my father did not worry too much about the ring, he felt he was lucky to be alive and, as for the Chetnik leader who had tried to murder him, he probably sold it on which would make it almost impossible to trace. The episode became a family story which was recounted from time to time when I was growing up and that was all."

Luigi gently stubbed out his cigarette and dropped it in the ashtray.

"But he never forgot his name."

"Don't tell me" I said, "Tito."

"No - Taveric."

" Donetta's Grandfather?"

"Great Uncle, her uncle's father."

"And you believe that Donetta's ring is the one

stolen from your father."

"My inquiries lead me to suppose it is, but I may be mistaken. If she showed it to me I would know. I would even be prepared to pay a reasonable sum for its return." He handed me a card. "You can reach me at this number. Phone me as soon as you have contacted her and we can set up a meeting."

"I have to go to Paris tonight" I said, but I will give her your message and your card. If you are happy to wait for a few days, I will be back in London after the week-end."

"I would advise you to tell her to sort this out immediately, later might be too late." He stood up. "As the eldest son, it is my duty to do this for my father. He will rest easier in his grave." On this heartwarmingly sentimental note he left.

I poured myself another whisky from the bottle on the table and glanced at his card. Printed on one side were the words the Dubrovnik Hotel, an address and a phone number, the other side was blank. I put it in my pocket.

I hadn't originally been going to Paris that night, but there was no way I was going play patsy for him and Donetta. I had been the fifth wheel in this business for long enough. I would tell her about

Luigi's offer on my way to the night train and that would be it. The decision made me feel better which is something but, like a lot of decisions, it didn't have any bearing on what happened.

The weather had turned colder and it was freezing hard as I left the flat. I walked past a row of grim South London houses to the Pavement in Clapham's Old Town and round to the station. Despite the street lights the place had a depressed look, not helped by the massed darkness of the common on my right.

A blast of warm, dirty air hit me as I went down the stairs to the ticket office. Someone was slowly buying a weekly pass and, as I huddled impatiently behind him, I was annoyed to see a plump man in a neat raincoat buy a ticket at the machine with the correct change and disappear down the stairs towards the trains.

I didn't see him again until after I had changed at Victoria to take the district line to Earls Court. The train was just pulling in when I noticed the same neat, rain coated figure standing about ten yards away from me immersed in reading the details on a poster. I was still feeling enough like Humphrey Bogart to know I was being followed.

I got out at Earls Court and walked quickly back along the side of the train towards the exit. Passengers got on and off and the doors started to close. At the last second, I leapt back on and stood watching the platform as the train pulled out. The rain coated man was walking unconcernedly along ignoring everything around him. Feeling that maybe my nerves had got the better of me, I got out at West Brompton and started walking back down the Brompton Road to the Noire.

My boots rapped crisply against the frozen pavement. Behind the railings on my right lay the gravestones and mausoleums of Brompton Cemetery, silent and isolated under the city night sky. Beside me, in the road, a police car suddenly roared into life and accelerated away, siren blaring. Across the street, two drunks were arguing and a girl was crying.

I was nearing the Noire now. Looking up, I saw the wooden sign swaying in the wind. Suddenly, I quickened my pace. Arriving at the cafe, I tugged open the door and ducked in. I had just seen a rain coated man come out of a tobacconist's.

Inside, candles, conversation and coffee were going full blast. Leo was behind the counter morosely taking money hand over fist and serving people with ill concealed irritation. He greeted me by raising his eyes to Heaven. I went round the end of the counter and down into the kitchen to find Donetta.

She was standing in the middle of the floor, her black, low cut dress emphasising the beauty of her cream shoulders and cascading hair. She was laughing and declaiming loudly, imitating a customer who had somehow queried the service. Apart from being a lecher and bad mannered, he was also old, ugly and a 'stupid bastard'. Pascal was smiling at her antics while slicing up mushrooms for an omelette.

"Donetta!" I said, "I've got to talk to you."

She turned, head back, arms outstretched.

"Peter!" she yelled, "have a glass of wine."

Swirling decoratively to the work top by the cooker, she grabbed a bottle of Bulgarian red, poured out a glass and, taking a gulp in passing, handed it to me. Then she dashed upstairs carrying two salads and a soup. I drank the wine and leant against the sink, drumming my fingers.

Three minutes later, she was back with more orders and I tried again. This time she listened, looking at me with attentive severity and chewing her underlip. I told her of Luigi's offer and also that I thought I was being followed.

"A reasonable sum, pph! These people think they are dealing with a peasant. I will teach them, I have other sticks in the fire."

"Irons."

"Huh?" She looked at me abstractedly, her mind racing.

"Listen Peter, there is no time to be wasted, you must speak to Ivan."

"I can't, I am going to Paris tonight to meet some musicians for Zollenhorn. I just came here to let you know what was happening and to tell you again, for what it is worth, get rid of that bloody ring. Send it back to your uncle, give it to Ivan, or whatever you like, but get rid of it."

She suddenly seemed to focus on me. It was almost as if she was seeing me for the first time. She leant forward to pick a thread off my shirt front and said: "You are right Peter, I will go and get it when I finish work, but what about that guy you think is following you?"

"I will go upstairs and see if he is there. If he is, I will have a coffee as if I am waiting for you. You come up after a minute or two, take some orders and tell me you will be finished in about half an hour. Then go back down to the kitchen and leave by the rear door. I will give you five minutes start and then go for my train, which," I glanced at my watch, "I might still make."

She smiled emotionally. "Thanks Peter, I won't forget this."

The man in the raincoat was sitting near the door, a mug of frothy coffee in front of him, staring at a guttering candle. I bought a coffee for myself and sat down to wait.

The room hummed with conversation. Aging arty types and young foreign girls mingled with students and slightly exaggerated sophisticates. At the next table, two cosmopolitan Australians argued about the relative merits of Berlin and Vienna, then spoiled the effect by each trying to get the other to pay for his coffee.

Donetta came up to take an order. She turned to me, ostentatiously pointed to ten o'clock on her watch and disappeared. I tried to look bored and relaxed. Miles Davis doodled from the speakers.

Five minutes later I got up, picked up my overnight bag and left. The man with the raincoat did not look up and didn't follow me out. That meant either he was after Donetta, or he was an innocent bystander. I hailed a taxi and jumped in. I had ten minutes to get to Victoria.

Everything went like clockwork. I ran onto the platform just as the train was beginning to move. I jerked open a door, threw in my bag and leapt in after it. Behind me a voice yelled: "Wait! Don't close it."

Next second a small, black coated figure with a mane of fair hair scrambled in beside me. Donetta.

"I didn't think I would make it" she said, pushing the hair out of her eyes.

"Well you did" I said, "but why?"

"Because" she replied, "handing me her bag to throw on the rack and collapsing onto a seat, "I wanted to go to Paris."

"I thought you were going to see Ivan" I hissed, "and get rid of the ring."

She leant forward and her eyes flickered round the carriage. There were no passengers near.

"Ivan" she whispered, "is dead."

11 MURDER

The train rattled into the night passing incoming trains half empty, the passengers framed in squares of light moving through the darkness. I reached for my cigarettes, then remembered we were in a non smoker. At first I felt nothing at what Donetta had told me. It was like a newspaper report, something you deal with by not dealing with it. Tragic yes, but it did not concern me. Murder, torture and destruction, things I had never seen, were as familiar to me through the media as breakfast cereal. This was just one more statistic.

I looked at Donetta. She was tucked into the corner seat, her forehead against the window, watching the suburban debris drift by in patches of streetlight and shadow. I saw that the initial adrenaline reaction had worn off and shock was beginning to set in.

"Tell me what happened" I said.

She turned towards me. There were tears in her eyes and she plucked at a crumpled handkerchief which she was holding in her hand.

"I was so frightened. I had to get away. I couldn't think of anything else. You were leaving for Paris and I would be alone. I just grabbed my passport, threw a few things into a bag and raced for the station."

Yes, but before that, how did you discover that he was dead?"

"I left the Noire as we planned and went to where I am staying. It is one of those big blocks of old red brick flats near the Earls Court Road. It is an expensive place with a wide carpeted hall, shell wall lights and a lift. The flat is on the first floor. Everything was quiet and the door was locked as normal.

"I let myself in and switched on the light. Nothing happened. I assumed a bulb had gone and felt my way over to the desk lamp by the window. A hanging plant brushed my face and I barked my shin on a chair, so by the time I had reached the desk and pressed the light switch I was already jumpy. I pulled the curtain across the window and turned round. He was slumped in a chair by the cold fireplace, as if he had been thrown there. The back of his head had been smashed in - there was blood everywhere. I could tell by what I could see of his face that it was Ivan."

"Did he know you were staying there?"

She gave a deep shrug and spread her hands wide.

"I don't see how he could."

"I suppose it wouldn't be difficult" I mused. "It is an area you frequent. You could easily be followed without you knowing it."

"But who would want to kill him, and why do it in my room? Whoever it was must have known he was coming and lain in wait for him, because I noticed that the bulb hadn't blown, it had been removed."

That sounded ominous, but I didn't say anything. The door opened at the end of the carriage and the guard came through checking tickets. I expected him to read the drawn, hunted looks on our faces and know us for murderers, but he punched the tickets without a glance and moved on.

"Why didn't you phone the police? I asked. I tried to keep my voice low, but the words seemed to echo through the train.

"I was scared. I had to talk to someone and the only person I could think of was you. My first thought was to catch you at Victoria and stop you leaving, then it struck me that I had the necessary papers and I could go too. I wanted to pretend I had never been at the flat. Unless someone noticed me go in and I don't think anyone did, there is no reason why I shouldn't say I went straight to the station to meet you."

"Forget it. Stick to the truth, if you want to stay out of trouble." It would be a new concept for her, but I thought I would throw it into the hat for what it was worth. "How soon will the body be discovered?" I continued.

"The flats are serviced. I think the cleaner comes in tomorrow."

"Who owns the flat?"

"Geraldine, a friend of mine at the Noire. She often stays with her boyfriend, so she said I could stay there for a few days."

"Can you contact her?"

Donetta shrugged and flicked her hand."

"I suppose so, I have got her number. She won't go to the flat. Why all these stupid questions? Don't you understand? Ivan has been murdered and when the police find out, they are going to think I did it and his whole family will hate me and I will be killed and - poor Ivan..." She shuddered and pushed herself against the back of the seat, shutting her eyes.

I was starting to get a headache. I put my hand in my pocket for my cigarettes and took it out again. I thought of pulling the communication cord, or getting the guard to telephone back to London, but I knew I wouldn't. I did not want to let Donetta down and the idea of making a spectacle of myself by charging along the train yelling murder did not appeal. I listened to the rhythm of the train for a few moments, it sounded unreal and far away. I tried to be patient.

"Donetta, if you are going to break down, the place to do it is in a police station. You haven't committed a murder and the police are not going to be stupid enough to think you have. You should report this straight away, the sooner they know the more chance they have of catching the real killer."

It was her turn to be patient.

"I know who did it, but I can't prove it and neither could the police. There will be no fingerprints and he will have been too careful to be recognised coming or going. This was done by the organisation you did not believe existed: The Burning Crown.

The black sea glimmered under the lights of Dover as the ferry pulled out into the channel. The wind was cold with the smell of salt spray and, apart from Donetta and me, the deck was empty. We stood on the more sheltered side, leaning on the rail, looking back at the rugged outline of the cliffs. We lit cigarettes and watched the smoke whip away into the darkness. I broke the silence reluctantly.

"No one can overhear us out here, tell me the full story as you should have told it the first time."

Donetta turned a pale tired face towards me. I felt cruel and insensitive.

"You know I have agreed to send the ring back, so this is over but, if you take something that belongs to you as much as to anyone else, it is not stealing. I knew my uncle wanted me out of the way and I did not see why I should be pushed around for nothing."

"So where did you get the ring?"

"I went to my uncle's office, as I told you, and told him what I had seen in the crypt, thinking he would protect me. He tried to pretend incredulity at my story, but I could see that he was worried. 'My little niece has a big imagination' he said, leaning back in his chair and laughing. 'Croatia is moving towards democracy, government is becoming more open and accountable. Respectable people like these you mention have no need to hide in damp corners to discuss their ideas. I would happily phone them now to put your mind at rest, but I know they would think you a lunatic, and probably me too. The best thing I can do is get you away from Jan's influence for a couple of months. You can carry out a little commission for me at the same time.'

"He went over to an ornate cabinet on one side of the room and pressed something. A hidden drawer popped open and he took out a small, black velvet bag.

"'Here' he said, letting the contents slide into my hand, 'take this and deliver it to the Dubrovnik Hotel in London, ask for Harvac. I will give you the address.'

"I looked down and there was the ring. My heart gave a leap of surprise and satisfaction. He did not know that I had ever seen it before, but I had. I had been wondering where it had disappeared to for years.

"When I was a child I used to visit my grandmother who lived in a large flat near the market square. I remember tall windows, a marble fireplace and dark heavy furniture. To someone who lived in a modern, purpose built, concrete high rise on the other side of the Sava, it was a place of romance and mystery. My grandmother had married before the war and could tell stories of the old Croatian high society. She had aristocratic and gypsy blood and must have been very beautiful as a young girl.

"I remember sitting beside her on winter afternoons watching the firelight shadows flicker on her lined, hawk like face. Hour after hour her dark eyes held me spellbound as she recounted old folk tales and stories of magic, ghosts and vampires. She was like a benign witch.

"One day, when I was about six or seven, she showed me the ring. She said it had belonged to Kings and Queens and, through history, it had moved between death and prosperity, as if its landscape was a checkered board, like the red and white squares of the Croatian shield.

"I asked her where she had got it.

'An Austrian prince gave it to me for some help I

was able to give his family during the war. Here, try it on.'

"I slipped it on my finger and held it up to the light, admiring its beauty. My Grandmother laughed.

'So the little princess (she called me her princess) has good taste. Well it should belong to royalty, maybe one day it will be yours.'

"I never saw it again, but I never forgot her words. When she died the ring never came to light. Now here I was in my uncle's office being told to give it to someone in London.

"I was to take it to a man named Harvac. Apparently, it was a part of his family's art collection which had been confiscated under Tito. 'He has been helpful to our government' my uncle said, 'and we agreed on this concession. I will contact him in the meantime and arrange for him to give you some English currency on its receipt.'

"Of course, I did not believe a word of this, but I took the ring and came to England."

"But you never went to Harvac."

"No, I considered that my grandmother had given it to me. One thing I was sure of: it didn't belong to this Harvac. I thought that if I kept the ring and he kept the money we would be all square."

I threw my cigarette butt over the side and watched it arc down into the water. If it were not for Ivan's death, this would just be the story of a corrupt official picking the wrong middle woman for his foreign currency racket. The murder showed it was something more serious.

'The ring is worth more than Harvac would have given you" I said, "your uncle was probably using you to get some cash out of the country and at the same time giving you spending money."

"I know." She wrinkled her nose mischievously. "But my uncle makes plenty of money, he could stand to lose a little on the ring."

"Who is Harvac anyway? Do you know anything about him?"

"No, I will send him the ring, then they can carry on and be happy. Come on, it's cold. Let's have some coffee."

12 PARIS

It was nearly seven o'clock in the morning when we walked out of Gare de Nord station. A soft, grey drizzle gave a damp glisten to the awakening streets and the smell of newly baked bread hung in the air.

The New Day Ensemble was arriving at St. Lazare at three the next day, so we had thirty hours to kill. I remembered a cheap hotel in the Rue Dauphine and hailed a taxi.

The taxi driver, untidy, round faced and bored, listened to my French without expression. Then he took off through the half empty streets like a scalded cat, slumped in his seat and apparently half asleep.

The Rue Dauphine is a narrow street on the Left Bank leading diagonally away from the Seine and the Hotel Mazarin is near the St. Germain end. The porter, who had been dozing in a chair, got slowly to his feet and dug out the register. He glanced at

Donetta sadly when I asked for two rooms. It seemed to sum up the essential tragedy of life for him, but he mastered himself sufficiently to hand over two keys and we went upstairs.

Our rooms were on the third floor. I paused before the door to mine and gave Donetta her key.

"We had better get a few hours sleep" I said.

She took the key and moved down to her door. As I let myself into my room, I realized she had hardly said anything since we had got on the train at Calais.

My room had a double bed, a wash basin and a shower with a plastic concertina door. The window looked out over the Rue Dauphine. I threw my bag on to a chair, took off my jacket and shoes and collapsed onto the bed. Sounds came up from the street below. The curtains shifted slightly at the open window. The wallpaper became comfortably blurred. I was lazily drifting off to sleep when I heard a gentle knocking at the door. I rolled onto my feet and opened it. Donetta was standing there holding a cigarette.

"I've run out of matches" she said.

She followed me into the room and sat down on the bed while I handed her a lighter.

"Is your room all right?" I asked.

"Fine."

I put an ashtray beside her and sat on the other side of the bed with my back against the head board. I did not know what to say, so I silently watched her smoke. Suddenly, she stubbed the half smoked cigarette out and turned to me.

"Pete, do you mind if I lie down here? It's just I don't want to be alone."

"Not at all."

"Thanks" she said, kicking off her shoes and swinging her legs onto the bed, "I knew you would understand." Expelling a quiet contented sigh, she turned over and tucked her arm through mine, like a child afraid I would go away. In a few moments, she was asleep.

I awoke a couple of hours later and, without moving, tried to look at my watch. It was ten to eleven. My arm had gone numb and I flexed my fingers to try and generate some circulation. I looked down at Donetta. She was breathing easily, her lips slightly parted, her hair flowing over the pillow. I could smell its fragrance.

What, I wondered, was I to do with her? I should have told the police the full story of the burglary, but

I hadn't. I had helped her hang on to what she admitted was stolen property. She had discovered a murder and I had let her leave the country. To top it all, her life was under threat. I was pretty sure she had been the real target when they had got Ivan. It was the only way it made sense. And, if they found out she was with me, I wouldn't last long either.

I heard a murmur beside me. Donetta disengaged her arm and stretched, screwing up her face and opening one eye.

"Hello."

"Hello" I said, extracting my arm and waving it about to try and shake some life back into it. "Feel better?"

"I think so, as soon as I wash my face I'll know."

"Good, we'll find a cafe and get something to eat, then you have to phone England."

The day was bright and cold. We crossed the Boulevard St. Germain at the Odeon and walked up past the university to the Rue Mouffetard. I needed the exercise and I wanted to clear my head. Market stalls lined both sides of the street and a busy self involved crowd of shoppers moved in ordered chaos all around us. Everyone seemed to have a place, a job to do, or a purpose for being there. I felt a twinge of envy, I had never felt as much at home anywhere as these people appeared to be, going about their daily lives.

We found a small cafe and had an omelette and a coffee each. After an initial burst of gaiety, Donetta had once more become morose and introspective.

"I can't get Ivan out of my mind" she said, "you don't know what it is like to discover someone dead, even someone you dislike. I feel sick when I think of it."

"That is why you cannot let whoever killed him get away with it. You have to contact the police."

"What is the point? He will have been found by the cleaner this morning and when Geraldine tells them I was staying at her flat, it will be me they will be after."

"Just tell the truth. You panicked and ran."

"They will wonder whether or not to believe me after they put me in jail."

"If you don't, you will only make things worse."

"All right, I'll phone, but I hope I never have to go back to that flat."

There was a public phone box near the cafe and, after assembling our combined change, Donetta made the call. I watched her make animated conversation, then put the phone down and join me.

"Well, at least that's over."

"What did they say?"

"I did not try to get through to the police. I phoned Leo at the Noire and told him to tell them."

"He must love you."

She laughed, pleased at her easy solution to the problem.

"He hated it, but what could he do?"

"Did you tell him where you were?"

"No, I did not want to complicate things. Come on, let's keep moving, it's too cold to stand still."

We walked down the Boulevard St. Michel and then along the Seine. The pale, early November sun brightened the colours on the cafe awnings and warmed the green painted wood of the bookstalls. The Louvre loomed like a cultural accusation across the river, but I wasn't in the mood for paintings. I wanted to do something. Act instead of re-act. Here was this girl, caught in the web of her own deceit and I had done nothing to help save her from herself. I had to do some serious thinking and there was only one way to do that. I had steered her away from the river and we were now walking towards St. Germain de Pres. Suddenly, I saw what I had been looking for, the brown wood and glass frontage of a small bar.

"How about a drink?" I said.

Inside it was more spacious than you would have expected. It was clean, run down and the sort of place I like. I liked the cracked mural in pastel colours running along two of the walls. I liked the one customer muttering to the patron in murmured phrases and I liked the afternoon sun filtering through the window on to the empty tables. It was like a little section of the world that had slipped its moorings from time. Perfect for daytime drinking. I ordered a bottle of vin ordinaire and we sat by the window.

"Do you know Mike Zollenhorn?" I asked.

"Of course I do, he comes into the Noire and, as he knows Croatia well, he likes talking to me. Why?"

"Does he know your uncle?"

"He makes it his business to know government officials, that is how he makes his money."

"I thought he was just an art dealer."

"He is as far as I know, but it doesn't take a genius to work out that you can't take paintings and valuable objets d'art out of a country like old Yugoslavia unless you either know people, or you are a good smuggler."

"This is beginning to make sense."

"No it isn't because I never even saw him until I came to England and it was Jan who told me I might be able to get a job at the Noire. A friend of his had worked there one summer."

"So you think he is all right?"

Donetta raised her hands and voice at the same time.

"How the hell do I know" I'm not his accountant, I'm a waitress. He sometimes has apple strudel, likes brandy in his coffee and talks too loud - so have him arrested."

"Try some more wine. The great thing about drinking is that you can't talk while you are doing it."

"OK, there is no reason for me to get angry, but what are you trying to say?"

"As I see it there are two things you can do: come back with me and go straight to the police, or get on a train and keep going until you reach Zagreb. Then you can go to your uncle and get him to sort it out. He is not going to want to hurt his niece."

"Maybe not, but he is not the only person in Zagreb. No, I can't do that."

"In that case, go to the police."

She looked at me and smiled.

"The touching British faith in the good old bobby." She paused. "The only problem is that, apart from the murder of Ivan of which I might well be accused, the only person who has committed a clearly provable crime is me. I will have to tell them I stole the ring."

"Leave that for the moment then. There is another possibility. Tell the whole story to Zollenhorn. He will very likely know, or be able to find out, the history of the ring. He can get in touch with your uncle and come to some arrangement - then you can go to the police."

"How do you know Zollenhorn?" she asked.

"He wanted someone to meet the New Day Ensemble. Giles suggested me and here I am."

"Quite a coincidence."

"It might be the stroke of luck we need."

"All right, I will go back with you to see him, although I don't suppose he will be able to do much."

It was after midnight by the time we got back to the hotel. We had wandered around the Latin Quarter, had a meal, another bottle of wine and a few brandies, so neither of us were feeling much pain.

Donetta came into my room for a last cigarette and reclined on the bed while I sat on a chair watching her. It may have been the drink, but I wasn't listening much to what she was saying. I was thinking how beautiful she looked with the gentle glow of the side lamp catching her golden hair and giving a warm glow to her skin.

Maybe, I thought, after all I had done for her, she was beginning to fall in love with me. I knew I was in love with her. The time and the setting seemed right. For a few moments I followed this cosy line of thought, then, gradually, out of my misty dreaming, there emerged before my mind's eye a picture of Claire giving her impression of Beatrice refusing Dante her greeting. I snapped back into reality and a little while later Donetta said goodnight.

13 THE NEW DAY ENSEMBLE

Lank, brown hair pulled sideways across a large head, dark brown eyes, a heavy moustache and a swarthy blue chin made up the face that topped a well filled black shirt, long winter coat and patent leather shoes. the whole creation stood beside a free standing cello case and made it look like an oversize violin.

"Nikolai Voinavitch" he said, pumping my hand up and down twice. The first time to show masterful dominance, the second to drop it dismissively.

"Zarina!"

A thin, pale girl, who had been mooning about aimlessly some distance away, wandered over. Her eyes were a luminous blue and her hair was so straight you would have thought there were weights hanging from the ends. Nikolai waved his arm majestically.

"Zarina Dabac, the flautist."

"Peter Delaney, St. Bernard" I said, taking her hand which melted away from mine as she gave it to me. "We leave from the Garre de Nord at seven" I continued, "I suggest we go over there now, find a restaurant near the station, have a meal and relax. We might be able to leave the instruments and bags at the left luggage."

"Our instruments are a part of us and never leave our side" said Nikolai, "but it would be a good idea to have something to eat."

Having made this pronouncement, he swung the cello on to his shoulder and marched off like a general leading a victory column into a defeated town. Zarina floated along behind him leaving me to pick up their two bags, mentally increasing the expenses as I did so.

Over the meal Nikolai grew more expansive. He seemed to fill the table with his presence and the restaurant with his personality.

"It is very sad" he said, tearing apart some bread and looking soulfully tragic at the same time. "Croatia is a country preparing to step into a great future and yet," he swallowed a bit of crust, "we have fighting, we have bombs, we have death.

People must reach into their souls. We have a history, we have a tradition, we have Art. These must not be forgotten and; therefore, these are what we," a depreciative shrug, "Zarina and I, hold up to them as in a mirror." He held up a large hand and peered at it intently. "Croatia faces Croatia. In our concerts, Zarina's and mine, we play for peace with our music as surely as any soldier fights for it with his gun.." He paused, reached for another bit of bread and shrugged. "One lives - one contributes."

"Do you know Leon Taveric?" I asked.

"Taveric, Taveric." Nikolai clicked his fingers as if to say here was something that might be familiar, but it eluded him. He turned to Zarina.

"It is not an uncommon name." Her voice was low and throaty and came unexpectedly from the pale serious face. "Why do you ask?"

"He is something to do with the administration in Zagreb and, as he has something to do with the Arts, I thought you might have dealt with him."

"If we have it would be in his official capacity and I would not necessarily remember his name. Do you know him?"

"No, he is the uncle of a friend of mine. You will be meeting her later, she wanted to visit Samaritaine while she was in Paris."

"Really!" he yawned. His disinterest was monumental.

I yawned back and looked at my watch. We still had an hour to waste before the train left.

I paid for the meal and we went over to the station bar where were were going to meet Donetta. I bought a round of beers and Nikolai went into a long monologue about how he hated flying and why he refused to put his cello in the hold and lots more in a similar vein. Finally, Donetta turned up. She was wearing dark glasses and a broad brimmed, black felt hat. I introduced her and we started for the train.

"I bought these things because I am nervous of going back through customs" she whispered.

"What are you going to do? Draw sunglasses and a hat on your passport photo?"

She gave me a dig in the ribs.

"Well, I might need them when I get to London."

Dover at six o'clock in the morning was dark and cold. As 'Road Manager' I carried the cello and did the talking. The boat train was in and we climbed into a cold compartment and sat and shivered. Donetta noticed a policeman on the platform and watched him like a hypnotised rabbit until the engine rumbled to life and we rolled out of the station.

When dawn broke we were rushing through the Kent countryside, past ploughed fields, oast houses, hedges and trees with their few remaining late autumn leaves hanging damp in the morning mist. Nikolai became expansive.

"England" he breathed, "home of democracy."

"Or was it Athens?" I said.

"Greece! - Greeks, what do they know about democracy? Ask the Macedonians." He laughed and winked at Zarina.

"We must get to Oakwood as soon as possible" he continued, "the concert is this evening and we need time to rest and prepare."

"There is a train to Exeter from Paddington at nine thirty," I said. "We will be met at the station and driven to Oakwood. You should be there early afternoon."

At Paddington I bought a paper, but could find no mention of the murder. I took Donetta with me when I went to get the tickets and told her to phone Leo. She came back a few minutes later, biting her underlip and looking puzzled.

"Leo is very annoyed" she said, "he thinks it was

a hoax. The police went to the flat and found nothing. The place was spotless and there was no Ivan."

14 OAKWOOD

A Range Rover met us at the station driven by Charles, an unctuous, balding man in his mid forties who turned out to be the cook. On the way back he divided his conversation equally between spiritual enlightenment and cookery. Rice, lentils and pasta seemed to be the backbone of his cuisine. It was obvious that the Oakwood menus were designed to sound good, but cost little.

After about half an hour, he turned into a narrow track which wound through overgrown grass and rambling hedges down to a late nineteenth century house. In front of the house the track widened into a gravelled sweep, encircling a magnificent cedar. A few people were strolling around the grounds.

He pulled up at the front door and we unloaded into a spacious, wood panelled hall containing low lighting, paintings and leather settees. Here we were met by Anthea the 'Artist Relations and Event Co-ordinator' and Charles retreated, presumably to his prayer mat, or his kitchen.

Anthea had arranged for the New Day Ensemble to stay at the house. Donetta and I were assigned to one of the cottages in the grounds. As soon as this had been settled, Nikolai and Zarina retired upstairs to rest while Anthea explained to us the order of business.

"Mr Zollenhorn will see you in his office at six o'clock to sort out payment for the trip. You are, of course, welcome to stay for the week-end as his guests. I am sure you will love it, if you do. We have some wonderful things on the programme. But I won't keep you any longer, no doubt you are dying for a wash and brush up. Dinner at seven, the concert starts at eight."

The sound of a doodling saxophone backed by free form percussion greeted us as we walked through the open cottage door. As I threw down my bag, I realised who it must be.

"Hey Jazzology!" I yelled.

A door opened and Isaac's curly head emerged.

"Pete, you actually got to Paris and back. Where's

the guide dog?"

"Isaac, let me introduce you to Donetta."

He leaned forward and shook her hand.

"Come in" he said, "you know Rico, don't you, Pete?"

"Yes" I said. Rico was a small, self contained Peruvian and the other half of the duo. We moved into the kitchen to make coffee.

"So, what's new?" asked Isaac.

"Ivan has been murdered."

"Christ! Well at least that means the police are handling it now."

"No, Donetta discovered the body, but she panicked and went to Paris with me without telling anyone. Later, she phoned Leo, who told the police, but by the time they got there the body had disappeared. Naturally, they suspect a hoax and, no doubt, Leo was happy to mention Donetta."

"Naturally."

"But before she talks to them the problem of the ring has to be sorted out. That is why I have decided to take your advice and see if Zollenhorn can help. I am meeting him at six o'clock to collect my cheque."

"Why should he help?" asked Rico, "I wouldn't

trust him with an empty wallet. This place has a strange vibe. I was up in the woods this morning and saw this guy dodging about in the trees. I thought he was staking the place out."

"Not a chance" laughed Isaac. He was just one of the crazy nuts staying here for the week-end pretending to be outdoor types. There is a family camping in the lower field with a wigwam and a Toyota truck. You can't get further back to nature than that."

"You don't understand" I explained, patiently, "Zollenhorn knows the scene, he even knows Donetta's uncle through his art dealings. He will know the value of the ring and he will probably be able to verify its true ownership. Apart from that, it might be a good idea for Donetta to have a respectable businessman on her side when she goes to the police."

"OK" said Rico, "It's your deal."

At six o'clock I went along to the office. It was a large, high ceilinged room made intimate by the use of lamp lighting. The effect was helped by a richly patterned Turkish carpet and dark oil paintings, hung low on the wall. Zollenhorn was sitting at his desk in a pool of light cast by a lamp.

"Ah Pete" he said, looking up. "It all went well I see. Sit down, I will be with you in a second."

He signed some papers and threw them in the out tray while I pulled up a chair and sat down.

"Now" he said, taking a large cheque book from a drawer, "how much do I owe you?"

I handed him an itemized bill for £400, which he glanced at casually before pulling out a red Moroccan leather wallet and counting out eight fifty pound notes.

"Here you are" he said, handing them to me, "I really appreciate you stepping in at such short notice. I hope you are going to be able to stay for the week-end."

"Thanks, I would like to" I said, putting the money in my pocket. "There is something else I wanted to discuss with you, if you've got a minute?"

"Certainly." He leaned back in his chair. "Fire away."

"I have a friend with me - Donetta Taveric. She knows you slightly."

The great man's brow furrowed for a second, then cleared.

"Oh, the little waitress at the Noire. Yes, her uncle

and I have business dealings occasionally, so I try to keep a friendly eye on her for his sake. What has she been up to?"

"She has got into a bit of trouble and I thought you might be able to advise her, maybe clear things up with her uncle before she goes to the police."

"Police!" Zollenhorn raised an eyebrow. "I am an art dealer, I have very little knowledge of the law. She should go to a solicitor. As for her uncle, I don't know him well and I make it a rule never to interfere in family matters."

"I understand that, but you do know Croatia and you do know jewellery. I don't expect you to get involved, all I want is your opinion."

I related the story from the first burglary to the murder and Donetta's flight to Paris. When I had finished, Zollenhorn laughed softly.

"Incredible, you must wonder how you got mixed up in something so bizarre. If we were wise, we would phone the police now, but like you I can't stand by when someone is in trouble, I have to do my best to help. Have you got the ring?"

"No Donetta has it. I will bring it along to show you tomorrow morning, if that is convenient?

"Certainly, it might be from a famous collection,

in which case it would be well documented. You see Croatia is in a state of flux, as is the rest of old Yugoslavia, and this has given rise to powerful new criminal elements willing and able to take advantage of the unstable situation. Croatia is being robbed of its heritage and it is almost impossible to keep track of the looting. So, if this ring is valuable, it is a serious criminal offense to have stolen it."

"She doesn't feel she has stolen it, she feels that it was in the family and her uncle had no right to sell it."

He opened his hand as if to say 'well whatever' and carried on.

"You don't know that he was going to sell it. It may have been no more than a pledge to Harvac in return for him giving Donetta some living expenses. Nevertheless, you would have thought that he would have written to her, or phoned her, or even asked me to get in touch with her before sending an undercover man after her - if he did?"

"Well Donetta is convinced he did send Ivan, but I can't see where Luigi fits in. How did he hear that Donetta had got the ring?"

"Don't worry, he is from Trieste. I have friends in Trieste who will be able to check him out for me."

I stood up. "That could be helpful" I said, "and Donetta will bring the ring over to show you tomorrow around nine."

"Good, I will be here in the office. It will be interesting to see what this silly girl has risked her life to hold on to."

Dinner was laid out as a buffet in the dinning room. The guests moved to and fro helping themselves to the food with jocular determination - everybody having fun and roughing it for charity at the same time. Jazzology were playing in the main hall, the discordant notes drifting into the room like musical indigestion. But it would have taken a lot more than that to put the caring bourgeoisie off their rice and salad. The snatches of conversation and the rattle of knives and forks grew louder, sounding far more avant-garde than anything Isaac and Rico could do.

After the meal, Donetta and I went out on to the wooden verandah that ran along one side of the house for a cigarette.

"Have you discussed any of this with Zollenhorn before?" I asked her.

"I would have no reason to - why?"

"He said Luigi was from Trieste. I only referred

to him as Italian, I never mentioned Trieste."

"You probably did, but forgot."

"No, it was deliberate. I told the whole story leaving out minor details knowing that, if he was already familiar with any of it, he might easily slip up."

"So all that stuff about asking him for help was just bullshit."

Not necessarily, but there were too many coincidences to take him completely at face value. For instance, he goes to the Noire, he knows your uncle and he deals in art from Eastern Europe. And hiring me to go to Paris was crazy. He either wanted me out of the way for a couple of days, or he thought that it would be easier for Nikolai and Zarina to get through customs if I was with them."

"And how would he even have heard of you?"

He could have heard about me from Ivan or Luigi. Giles recommended me for the job, but it wouldn't have been hard to manipulate that, he just had to ask him if he knew any music agents. The point is, did he get me out of the way to make it easier to kill you? Because it is obvious that whoever killed Ivan was really after you."

"For Christ's sake, Peter" Donetta's voice was a

strained whisper, "I hope you are just trying to scare me."

"You two will catch your death out here." The voice echoed loudly in the darkness. I turned to see Zollenhorn standing by the open French window, about to light up a cigar.

"I don't often get the chance to breathe real country air" I said, "so I like to dilute it with smoke."

He laughed politely. "I am as bad as you, I'm afraid. We are very keen on health down here, so there is no smoking in the house, but there is nothing like a good cigar after a meal." We smoked in silence for a minute or two, then he launched what remained of the cigar over the verandah rail and turned to go in. "The concert is due to start. I think Nikolai and Zarina deserve our support. It is wonderful what they are doing for their country."

I didn't know what they was doing, or who they was doing it for, but I was interested to see what their show was like. We slipped in at the back of the dinning - now music - room as Nikolai was starting his introduction.

"Ladies and gentlemen, we come to you from the war torn city of Zagreb. Old Yugoslavia is giving its death rattle and it is the rattle of machine guns and bombs. The bestiality of the Serbs allied to the complacency and ignorance of the West would be leaving a country of widows and orphans were not the widows and orphans being slaughtered as well.

"Bosnia is in peril, Albanians are suffering, parts of Croatia are under siege. So is the situation hopeless? Must we stand idly by while our fellow countrymen annihilate each other? No, ladies and gentlemen, the answer of the New Day Ensemble, Zarina's and mine, is a compassionate, but determined, No!

"Hearts must be awakened to higher things than a thirst for blood, or a lust for gold. Art must re-establish itself in the soul of the nation. We, Zarina and myself, are attempting in our own small way to assist in this process. From war torn Zagreb we bring you a message of peace. From you we hope to bring back your desire for peace in our hearts and your donations towards this vital work in our pockets."

A gentle ripple of applause flickered round the hall as Nikolai bowed and reached for his cello. He seated himself while Zarina, who had been sitting dove like at the side of the stage, rose to her feet and joined him. The concert began.

Renditions of Croatian folk songs, little bits of Bach and long sonorous pieces of their own composition followed. Nikolai was a player who believed that expression equalled vibrato and he gave it plenty of expression. Zarina ebbed and flowed beside him like a snake charmer without a snake. The audience dozed in their seats and mentally congratulated themselves on being so cultured.

After the concert, the guests dispersed to bed like mist on a June morning and Donetta and I went back to the cottage. Isaac and Rico were in the kitchen recovering from their earlier performance by drinking Bordeaux. They had got through a bottle and a half and had two more to go. I put a half empty bottle of duty free brandy on the table and we sat down.

"Zollenhorn has agreed to look at the ring tomorrow morning" I said.

"Good" said Isaac, pouring out two more glasses of wine.

"Not so good, he knows more about it than he should. We either have to get out tonight, which would leave us back where we started, or I have to break into his office and try and get some hard evidence of his involvement."

Rico leaned forward and looked at the brandy bottle.

"How much have you had to drink?" he said.

15 JAN

I left the cottage around twelve thirty. The grey, overcast day had cleared to a cold, moonlit night. Ahead of me, the house was in darkness, except for a light over the front door. I kept to the shadows as much as possible, in case some insomniac was keeping a lonely vigil by one of the windows.

At the end of the drive I ducked across to the verandah, Zollenhorn's office was at the back of the house on that side. I couldn't risk the boards on the verandah, so I pushed my way slowly through the damp bushes below the rail until I was opposite his window. There was a light on. Zollenhorn was still working.

I felt painfully visible with the moonlit fields behind me and the glow from the curtained window in front. If anyone came along it would be a miracle if I wasn't seen and yet I was learning nothing.

Someone laughed in an upstairs room and an owl hooted from the nearby trees. I stood there like an idiot, feeling damp and cold.

Then I noticed a gap at the top of the curtains where they were not quite drawn together and there was a small ventilator in the top centre pane. I had to get up there. I eased myself over the rail and on to the verandah. A board creaked and I froze. Ten seconds passed, but nothing happened. In two more strides I had reached the window. Very slowly, I climbed on to the narrow ledge, keeping my balance by pressing the palms of my hands against the brick inset. Finally, I was standing straight up and able to look through the gap into the room.

Zollenhorn was leaning over his desk looking down at something. Nikolai was seated in a chair watching him. A third person was sitting in a chair with his back to me.

"A piece of cake" Nikolai was saying, "Delaney carried the cello through and no one even looked at us. I believe it is a fine example."

"Yes - if it is genuine. These icons are becoming so popular that forgeries are common. I will have it examined."

"I took the risk bringing it in. I don't want to be

held up by any delays over payment."

"If you imported a fake there was no risk and your cut of nothing is nothing." Zollenhorn sneered as he walked over to a silver tray on which was a bottle of whisky and some glasses. It obviously amused him to emphasize the businessman's superiority over the mere donkey. He poured out three large whiskies, handed one each to the other two and carried his back to his desk.

"I will have to take it back to London to get it authenticated, then I will give you your money."

Nikolai swallowed half his whisky with relish and lit up a thin, black cigar. His dark eyes gazed sadly at Zollenhorn through the smoke.

"We return to Zagreb on Monday, but there is no problem. I will return the icon to Taveric and explain your lack of trust. I am sure he will understand."

Zollenhorn saw his little joke backfiring and didn't like it. A hard edge entered into his voice.

"It is up to me how I handle what Taveric sends and I have a reputation to uphold" His face relaxed into a smile. "Nevertheless, we have been friends for a long time and I know the difficulties he is working under at the moment. I will personally underwrite your fee with my own money. After all…" He looked up. "What was that?"

It was me. I had slipped while trying to redistribute my weight more comfortably. This was no time to hang about. Quick as a flash, I vaulted back over the rail and crouched in the bushes. I just made it before the curtain was whipped aside and a face peered out. It was my old pal Luigi. In a moment Zollenhorn had joined him.

"Probably a cat" I heard him say, "but go out and have a look around."

I started to panic. If there was one man I did not want to meet in these circumstances, it was Luigi, but there was a problem. If I tried to get away quickly, I would make too much noise going through the bushes, but if I stayed where I was, I would almost certainly be seen. I got down low trying to make myself as small as possible. I was nearly flat to the earth before I noticed it in the darkness. Part of the facing at the front of the verandah had rotted away, probably because of the damp of the bushes, leaving enough of a hole to roll under. I rolled under just as Luigi opened the doors of the French window and stepped through on to the boards above me.

Dead leaves, mould and a fetid smell, which I suspected was rats, surrounded me as I lay there listening to the measured tread of his boots. A torch played over the bushes where I had been only a few seconds ago. Then the steps seemed to move to the office window. A moment later, they turned and went back inside and the French window doors closed. I had got away with it.

I rolled out from under the verandah and began to slide carefully along through the bushes. I remembered how I used to love this sort of thing when I was a child, now I wouldn't have given you tuppence for it. When I reached the end of the house I stood up. I was pleased to notice that someone had switched off the lamp over the front door.

A torch flashed in my face.

"Predictable Mr. Delaney, much too predictable."

I couldn't see much with the torch shining in my eyes, but the voice told me that luigi's too solid form was right behind it. I felt stupid, annoyed and scared. Then, without me thinking anything at all, a strange thing happened. The resentment I had been harbouring for the past week burst to the surface in a rush of adrenaline.

I ducked under the light and hit low and hard. Luigi grunted and staggered back. Then the torch crashed against the side of my head, knocking me to the ground. I rolled over, sprang to my feet and lashed out blindly without connecting. I tried again and got him full in the face. He hardly faltered before countering with a karate punch to the throat which, luckily, was partly deflected by my chin. He followed this with another belt with the torch and I went down again. I began to feel that I was on the wrong side. I was out of breath, my head was humming and I could taste blood. As he moved in for the kill the Delaney fighting machine was temporarily out of ideas.

As it turned out I didn't need any. A black blur detached itself from the shadows and hit the Italian waist high, like a demolition ball broken from its chain. The two fell to the ground, scraping along the gravel. An arm went up and whipped downwards and Luigi lay still.

The figure leapt up and grabbed my arm.

"Come on." The accent was foreign. "We have to move fast."

We started running towards the cottage, using the grass so as to make less noise. They would find Luigi in a couple of minutes at the most and then all hell would break loose.

It took us about thirty seconds to get to the

cottage and I led the way into the kitchen. Rico and Isaac were both looking extremely mellow. Donetta was pouring out a glass of wine. She stood up when she saw who was with me, fear and then anger registering on her face. She snapped out something in Croatian which he replied to, equally abruptly, then he changed to English. "They will be here in a minute. We have to go, or innocent people will get hurt."

"Screw them, man" said Isaac, his voice was slightly slurred, "there are four of us here."

"No" I said, "as far as they know, you know nothing. Just tell them that Donetta and I went out about half an hour ago and you haven't seen us since. We can get out through the woods and go across country to the nearest village."

"I have a van parked not far away" said the stranger.

I turned and saw him properly for the first time. He was tall and slim and wearing a black donkey jacket, jeans and boots. His light brown hair was nearly covered by a black woollen army cap.

Donetta grabbed her coat and the three of us slipped out into the night, leaving Isaac and Rico washing the extra glasses and rearranging the chairs.

We ran through some scrub in front of the cottage, crossed a ditch and climbed through a barbed wire fence into a field. The moon had become obscured by cloud and we couldn't see much except the darker outline of the trees against the night sky. The field ran down to a stream behind which rose a wooded hillside.

When we got to the stream the stranger produced a pencil torch and guided us across from stone to stone. He switched it off again as soon as we were over and we climbed the bank to a narrow path. We crossed this and started to make our way up through the trees on the other side. It was a hard and noisy scramble through bramble bushes, fallen branches and dead leaves. After a minute or two, we stopped to catch our breath and I looked back over the way we had come.

Across the valley I could see the lamp, once more on over the front door of the house, casting a pool of light. Further along was the lighted kitchen window of the cottage. As I watched, the headlights of a car curled down the drive to the road and turned left out of the gate. A moment later another followed, turning right.

"They are sealing off the roads" said the stranger,

"but I don't think they have enough manpower to do it properly. We should still be able to cut across to my van."

I remembered that I didn't know who he was.

"Maybe we should introduce ourselves" I said, "I'm Pete."

"This is Jan" said Donetta, "it is his fault all this happened."

"You did not behave as I expected, but I suppose that was to be expected" laughed Jan.

"You set me up and you know it...wait - look!"

Two figures with powerful torches were crossing the field towards the wood. Jan pulled a gun from inside his jacket. He flicked off the safety catch. I could only see it glinting in the darkness, but I thought it was a Mauser, a German officer's pistol from the Second World War.

"This isn't Croatia" I said, "What we have to do is get back to London, not make a last stand. Those two are probably not even armed."

"I'm afraid you don't know who you're dealing with" said Jan.

"It doesn't matter. They would be lucky to find us up here at night."

"If we move, they will hear us and if we don't,

they have a good chance of picking us out with their torches. We are too near the path."

I knew he was saying this because of Donetta and me. If he was as well trained as he looked, he could have melted into the undergrowth like snow on a wet pavement.

"All right" I said, "You know these woods better than me, so you have to stay with Donetta. I'll draw them off down the path. After they have gone, you can take her across the hill to the road. I will work my way round and meet you on the other side in an hour or two."

I could see Jan didn't like it, but he knew it was the best solution. After all, his job was Donetta, she was the key to the whole thing.

"O.K." he said, "But take my gun."

"I won't need it "I said, and started half running, half sliding my way back down to the path. By now the two men were crossing the stream and one of them shouted when he heard the noise. I reached the path and took off like a headless chicken, making as much of a racket as possible. At the first turning I ran into a tree, and nearly knocked myself out. After that I was more careful. I remembered my childhood days as an Iroquois brave in the woods and fields around Canterbury and tried to behave accordingly.

The path curved back and forth, roughly following the river below. Even in daylight you could not have seen more than twenty yards along it in either direction. At night you were reduced to picking your way through black and less black sections of darkness. After two or three minutes of this, I stopped to listen.

A prickling sensation ran up my spine as I heard a thudding sound that wasn't my heart. Looking back I saw flickers of light glancing off the branches. They were running, and a lot faster than I could because of their torches. I slipped off the track on the river side and slithered down behind a tree. A moment later the footsteps were above me and I buried my face in the wet leaves and moss. I could feel the beams playing on the trees and bushes around me and I thanked God for my black leather jacket and faded black jeans. After a few seconds, I heard them take off again, but I didn't move. I lay there with the damp soaking into my shirt and the cold, lonely night still and silent around me. My plan was to out wait them. All I had to do was to keep down the noise of my chattering teeth and shivering bones.

Time passed, only the occasional rustle, or owl

hoot breaking the silence. It got colder and colder. I began to see my life stretching before me in a series of twilight days plagued with rheumatism, arthritis and pneumonia. Finally, I heard them coming back.

They were walking slowly along mumbling to each other in a language that sounded Eastern European. One was smoking a cigarette. They no longer seemed to be searching. That is the trouble, you can't get the staff these days. I watched them re-cross the river before I set about persuading my frozen muscles to move. Eventually, I got to my feet and climbed back up to the track. Now I had to find out where Jan and Donetta had got to. Wearily, I began to push my way up through the trees in what I hoped was the right direction.

.

16 THE RING'S SECRET

By now it was about two o'clock in the morning. Although I did not think I could be heard by anyone, I still tried to move quietly. Brambles tore at my hands as I felt my way forward and I must have stepped on every broken branch and twig in the whole wood. I stopped frequently to listen, but heard nothing except the whisper of the night wind and my own breathing.

I wondered how many people had been in the cars? Not more than two per car, I thought. Zollenhorn could not have anticipated this development and you don't need heavies to monitor a fund raising week-end. But maybe the house was used as a safe way to filter people in and out of the country. I tried to remember how many serious, self important faces in sharp suits I had seen around the place - none, as far as I knew.

Fifteen minutes slow, painful going brought me to the edge of the wood. The moon, partially obscured by a wraith of cloud, hung low in the sky. In front of me, twenty yards of open ground ran down to a dry stone wall and the road. A hundred yards along the road to the right I could see the outline of a parked car. I assumed this was one of the two cars I had seen leaving the house an hour or so ago.

Without leaving the shelter of the trees I studied the lie of the land. Nothing moved and nothing looked like itself, every shadow, every bush, every tree became a watching man, and the longer I waited, the worse it appeared. I gambled on my own capacity for self delusion and started to weave my way along the boundary of the wood.

"Peter, stop crashing about like a wounded elephant."

I turned and saw Donetta not more than five feet away, regarding me with mild amusement. Jan was a black shadow leaning against a nearby tree.

"The situation is this," he said. My van is parked on the other side of the road near where they have positioned one of the cars. The people in it will be armed and in contact with the house by mobile phone. That means we have to take them out before they have a chance to call for help."

"The only way is to get them out of the car on some pretext," said Donetta.

Nobody had any ideas. We stared at the fifty yards of meadow, the stone wall and the car, sitting silent and ominous. In an hour or two it would be dawn and then we would have as much chance as a butterfly on a pin.

I was looking along the line of trees to our left, back the way I had come, when I noticed a curve where a scattering of trees came out within a few yards of the road.

"If we used that cover to get into the shelter of the wall," I said, pointing, we could work our way back along to the car. Then Donetta and I jump the wall as if we are making a break for it. She falls, pretending she has twisted her ankle and can't move. They know we are unarmed, so they won't think twice about getting out of the car to pick us up. Jan waits till they are in the open, then covers them from behind the wall. We disarm them, take their mobile phone and disable the car. That should give us about twenty minutes head start. What do you think?"

"We will have to try it," said Jan.

"But what if they just start shooting?" asked

Donetta.

"You've had it," muttered Jan, as we made our way through the trees, "but don't worry, you won't die alone, I will see to that."

"Somehow, that fails to comfort me," said Donetta.

The wall was roughly four feet high and built with jagged stones, some of which had been blown or knocked onto the grass at its base. This made crawling behind it in the dark a painful business. Jan went first, working his way back until he was opposite the car. He wanted to be behind them when they got out. Once he was in position, he waved the Mauser to signal he was ready.

Donetta stood up, placed her hands on top of the wall and, with a lift from me, sprang up and over. As she hit the ground on the other side, she gave a pained cry and collapsed in a heap. I scrambled over after her. The next second we were caught in the glare of headlights. I heard the car doors open and two men came running towards us. I grabbed her arm.

"Get up for Christ's sake."

"I can't," she moaned, "I think I have broken my leg."

"Come with us." The voice was thick and guttural. There wasn't a trace of interest in either of their faces. They were wearing zip up leather jackets, jeans and trainers.

"She has sprained her ankle," I explained, "you will have to help me get her to the car."

The one who had spoken gestured to his companion to give Donetta a hand.

"Don't move!" Jan's voice rang out from the impenetrable blackness beyond the lights.

The two men turned slowly in the direction of the sound, drifting apart, casually, as if by accident.

A sharp crack shattered the stillness and echoed back from the trees before dying away.

"Scheisse!" The leader of the two men grabbed his thigh and keeled over, blood oozing through his fingers. The other stopped and raised his hands.

"Get their guns, Pete and don't stand in the line of fire."

I took their guns from inside their jackets, while Donetta ran down to the car.

"The mobile phone is here" she said. "Come on, let's go."

I jumped into the driver's seat, flicked the ignition switch and the car purred into life. Jan ran across the road and vaulted the wall into the field where his van was parked. He drove it out through an open gate a little farther along. I spun the car round the two men in a screech of tyres and we were gone.

Jan led the way through the narrow country lanes which he had obviously taken the trouble to study because he never hesitated at any of the vaguely directional sign posts. After ten minutes fast driving he pulled on to the grass verge and stopped. I jerked to a halt behind him and we got out.

"We'll leave their car here" he said, "they might give its number to the police."

Donetta got into the passenger seat of the van while I climbed into the back. There wasn't much in there except a pack. I propped it against one side and sat on it, trying to make my back as comfortable as possible against the van's vibrations. We soon hit the A road which took us through Totnes and on to the M5. I kept my eye open for a motorway stop. As far as I was concerned it was time for breakfast and hot strong coffee.

"When Zollenhorn hears about me," said Jan, after a long silence, he will put two and two together and assume it's him I am after. With any luck, the rest of the organisation will think so too." He turned to Donetta. "What instructions were given to you before you left Zagreb?"

"I was told to deliver the ring to a man called Harvac. He was supposed to help me with money and contacts."

"Where does he live?"

"He runs a hotel in Victoria."

"Right, we go to London and take it from there."

"First," I said, "let's have breakfast. There is a motorway stop a mile ahead. Also, it might be a good idea to sketch out a plan of action."

"Fine," said Jan, "I want to have a look at the ring anyway."

The services car park was nearly empty and there weren't many people in the restaurant. We filled our trays with bacon, eggs, toast and coffee and sat down. An elderly woman was pushing a trolley around collecting plates. If she had been told she was going to be shot after she finished, she couldn't have moved slower. A man was washing the floor on the same principle.

There was little conversation during the meal. I hadn't realized how hungry I was until I started eating and the other two didn't hang about either. When we had finished, I got some more coffees and

Jan asked to see the ring.

"The only valuable thing that has ever been given to me and half of Europe thinks they own it," she said.

Jan smiled thinly. "When you accused me of setting you up," he said, "you were right. But I did not mean to put you at risk. You must admit, though, that was your own fault."

'Uncle Leon was using me. I didn't see why I should help him illegally smuggle my ring out of the country, so I took it."

"Of course," said Jan, "but I don't think it is as simple as that. As you know, my father is a minister for the Croatian government. He is on the progressive side of the party. He wants Croatia to run her own affairs and he wants democracy, but not at the expense of the rest of Yugoslavia. However, not everyone in the government feels this way. There are huge fortunes to be made in a completely separate Croatia with re-established links between herself and Western Europe.

"During Tito's time a tight grip was kept on the ideological picture of the economy. To him this meant that various industries were distributed to the most needy places throughout the member states, not necessarily the place that was most cost effective, but the most cosmetic. This policy, bolstered by borrowing abroad, was administered by local despots who feathered their own nests and preferred to falsify the figures rather than let Tito know it was not working. When the Eastern Bloc broke up, this small group of survivors were in place and ready to take advantage of the situation.

"As you know, the Balkans were the overland gateway between the East and the West. It is not so important now for normal trade, but for the illegal side of the market it is sill big business. Drugs via Bulgaria, art from Russia and Hungary and people from Turkey and the East are being funnelled into Western Europe. And these local despots I have been telling you about earn big money by keeping their eyes closed to what is going on.

"So here we have a group of crooked politicians, more or less controlled by the underworld, who have banded together into a secret society primarily, perhaps, to protect themselves, but also to use their money and influence to take power."

"What can you do about it?" I asked.

"That is what I am here to find out." He turned to Donetta. "When you and I discovered evidence of the Sekta Uzarene Krune in the crypt under St. Marks, that was not the first time I had been there, as you know. I had stumbled on it a couple of days before. I discussed it with Ivan and we decided to try and put them under pressure in the hope that one of them would panic and do something stupid. What's wrong?"

I was feeling sick. So Ivan wasn't a cop, or a member of a new, ultra right wing Ustase.

"Ivan was working with you?" said Donetta. She didn't look very happy either.

"Yes, he and I have been friends since we did our national service together. He is now working for Intelligence." He paused. "Did you say was?"

"I am afraid so," I said, "he was killed two days ago. I think they were really after Donetta."

"I knew something was wrong. I have not been able to get in touch with him since I came." He stopped and stared out the window, his face looked lined and tired.

I made a big production out of pulling three cigarettes from a packet. I handed them round and lit up. Jan fiddled with his with his without lighting it.

"What happened?" he asked.

Donetta told him how she had found the body,

panicked and left for Paris, and how, by the time she had informed the police, the body had disappeared.

"It doesn't matter," he said, "I will find out who did it." He was looking at Donetta, but there was no contact in his eyes, they seemed to burn through her to something in the distance. She shifted uncomfortably.

"Here," she said, reaching into her pocket, "you wanted to see the ring."

He took it and began examining it closely.

"Interesting," he said, "do you know the significance of these letters A.E.I.O.U.?"

"We found out that much," I said. "It means the House of Austria shall rule the world and that means that it probably belonged to Frederick the Third."

"I see, of course these people have nothing to do with the Hapsburgs, but they like an historical basis to their hooliganism. That is the reason why the group in Croatia call themselves the 'Sekta Uzarene Krune' It gives an air of self righteousness and a sense of purpose to be aligned with an old peasant revolt."

"Failed," Donetta pointed out.

"Maybe, but it was Croatia for Croatians and we are all susceptible to that."

"That's all very well," I broke in, "but we still don't know why Donetta was given the damn thing."

"Not yet, but we know it is important. Ivan and I knew we had to stir things up, or it would be too late. Donetta was doing some stuff for Youth Radio and I knew she would be interested in a spooky story. I also knew she would run to her uncle, if I could scare her into it. I knocked her brooch off in the crypt, let her know some of the names involved and she was off like a trained seal."

"What a flattering picture you draw," said Donetta. "Did it occur to you I could have been killed?"

"You were in no danger if you had followed instructions. But that's beside the point, you were given this ring for a reason and we have to...Wait! Give me that brooch for a second."

"It hasn't got my name on it, so I suppose I am safe," she said as she handed it to him.

Jan took it without a word while peering at the niello workmanship around the jewel setting. Carefully, he pushed the brooch pin into a small hole in the design. The top sprang open. He turned it upside down over his palm and a tiny black disk fell out.

"What is it?" asked Donetta.

"A micro-dot," said Jan, smiling grimly as he lighted his cigarette, "now we're getting somewhere."

"But why go to all this trouble to send information in a micro dot when they could send it in a few seconds by fax?" I asked.

"Because a fax can be easily intercepted," said Jan, "and whatever is on here might be dynamite. Come on, we're wasting time."

17 JAN DISAPPEARS

By the time we reached London, commuter crowds were pouring out of Charing Cross Station. They moved like automatons, bristling with papers, umbrellas and mobile phones, on their way to give London's wheel of commerce another half-hearted turn.

Jan parked the van on a double yellow line in the Strand and went to the Charing Cross post office to look up the nearest micro-film service. Donetta was asleep in the passenger seat. I was standing on the pavement looking for suspicious characters.

For the last two hours on the motorway I had seen a tail in every car that stayed behind us for more than three minutes, now I was eyeing window shoppers who lingered nearby. My caution was unnecessary, the most serious threat was from a traffic warden and I did not see him until it was too late. I was throwing the ticket into the back of the van when Jan returned.

"There is one in Covent Garden. I will get the

film developed and see you at your place."

I gave him the address, then Donetta and I took the tube.

The flat had a strange air of unreality after the events of the previous few days. The furniture seemed cold and uninviting, like a house after a funeral and I noticed with surprise how tawdry and run down the paint work was. Donetta went to her room to try and reduce it to some semblance of order while I wandered moodily around pretending I was going to do some work. After ten minutes I had got close enough to sit down at the desk to check the answer machine. I was staring out the window listening to no messages when I heard Donetta come into the room. She leaned casually on my shoulder, her hair brushing my cheek.

"Pete" she said in a dreamily wondering voice, "What are we going to do?"

"About what?"

"About - you know – the ring. I mean, there is no reason why the ring should not be mine now, is there? Jan has got the micro film, Harvac or Luigi have no right to it and after what I have been through I deserve it. You could get it back from him, I'm sure you could. His father is rich anyway."

"You have more faith in my abilities than I have, because I don't think I could. If Jan succeeds in pinning all this on someone, and we are still alive, he is going to want it for evidence. As far as I'm concerned, if you never see the damn thing again you will be lucky."

She moved away from me, her eyes flashing anger from beneath contracted brows.

"But I won't forget it. It's mine. My family has owned it for generations. I won't live poor and dreary and have to fight everyday for pennies while someone else spends my money."

"That's a load of rubbish and you know it. You don't know who it belongs to any more than I do. If it is genuine, which I doubt, you can bet your life it doesn't belong to your family."

"Are you saying Grandmother was lying?"

"Well, she was your grandmother. But I don't think you would ever sell it anyway, it is to bound up with your romantic image of yourself - the beautiful, aristocratic, gypsy descendant of kings."

A hint of amusement flickered in her eyes.

"Suddenly you think you know me."

"I don't believe you are as avaricious as you pretend to be."

"You are wrong. I want security and I want to do things. I am fed up with everybody having money except me. It is different for you, a few drinks, a dream and your happy. You will never make any money peddling people like Giles and Isaac, but you don't care, it doesn't bother you to be second rate. I'm not like that. I had to grow up hard. I have had to fight for everything I've ever got. I come from a different world, half the time you British don't know you're born."

I looked at the old desk, the broken down settee and the dusty windows. It didn't say much for my side of the argument, but hell, I wasn't asking for a lifetime achievement award, I was trying to get her to see sense.

She lit a cigarette, blew smoke up into the air and tapped her foot.

"OK Peter, maybe you're right. Let's leave it. We can't do anything until Jan gets back anyway."

Evening came and Jan had still not turned up. The atmosphere in the flat was deadly. Donetta hadn't said a word to me since the argument and I had nothing to do except sit at the desk and pretend to be busy. At eight o'clock I got fed up, grabbed some contracts and left, telling Donetta that I had to take them over to Claire.

I went to the nearest pub and had a pint and a few whiskeys. Just standing there listening to the normal boring pub conversations burbling around me made me feel better. I had forgotten a real world existed. It was nice to know that South London's drinkers were nudging themselves towards oblivion in their usual way and that they could still sort out everyone's troubles but their own so easily.

Claire was surprised to see me.

"I thought you weren't going to be back till after the week-end," she said.

"Things became a little tense, so we left. But I'm sure Jan will sort it out."

"Who's Jan?"

I filled her in on the details.

"I don't believe it," she said, pouring Jasmine tea into two Chinese teacups, "I leave you to handle your own affairs for a couple of days and what happens? You manage to annoy half of Europe into trying to kill you."

"I know what I'm doing." Actually, I was in more of a fog now than when the whole thing started, but I wasn't going to admit that to Claire.

"When Jan finds out what is on that micro-dot," I continued, "We will know why these people wanted that ring and why they were prepared to kill to get it."

"Greed, probably – and fear, if they think you have found out anything. Come to think of it, Donetta was afraid of Ivan, maybe afraid enough to kill him."

"Are you suggesting that, in less than an hour, Donetta murdered a tall, strong, highly trained special agent, cleared up all traces, disposed of the body and met me at Victoria in time to catch the night train to Paris? She must be a magician."

"Or a witch," laughed Claire. "Seriously though, now that Jan is here you should back off. She doesn't need you and it is dangerous to be involved in things you don't understand. She seems mysterious to you, so you invest her actions with romance, but really she is no more than a thief."

"That is unfair and not worthy of you. Her background is different from ours. She has had to fight for everything she has got. Her country is in melt down. She's confused. We can't expect her not to want to get what she can out of life. Even if the ring was stolen by somebody at some point, she doesn't see owning it as dishonest."

Claire didn't say anything, she just looked at me as if I was a spider who had just been caught climbing out of the waste pipe into the bath. At first, I was puzzled. What had I done? Then I understood and I think I felt better than I had for about six months.

When I got back there was no Donetta. I immediately started to panic, cursing myself for leaving her alone. I was about to phone the police when I found the note on the kitchen work top. It said: I have decided to handle this on my own. Don't mess things up by trying to find me. Love Donetta.

After my defence of her to Claire, it seemed to put the icing on the cake. I tore up the note and went to bed.

18 THE NETWORK

The rattle of the letterbox jerked me awake. It was eight a.m. and broad daylight on a freezing cold morning. I threw on some clothes and went downstairs. A large brown envelope was lying on the mat. I took it up to the kitchen and slit it open.

A few sheets of paper, the ring wrapped in tissue paper and a hand written note slid out on to the work top. The note was scribbled in pencil: 'I am sending you the ring and a copy of the document, it is the whole network laid out from A to Z. I am going to check out Harvac. See you in the morning' It was signed Jan.

What whole network, I wondered, and what the hell possessed him to go and see Harvac on his own? I turned to the photocopies. They contained lists of names and addresses, plus itemised figures and totals, but it was written in Croatian, so it might have been holiday resorts or football results for all I knew. I could have kicked Donetta for disappearing just when she could have been useful. I made myself a cup of tea, sat down at the table in the dining area and thought about doing some work.

An hour later I was still sitting there staring at the cold sun coming through the window. I had gone over the story many times in my mind and I knew I was right, but somehow I didn't feel right. Once more I went over the facts.

1. At her own request, Donetta was no longer my concern. 2. Jan was a professional and the whole damn mess was probably his fault anyway. 3. Nobody wanted me to do anything and, besides, there was nothing I could think of to do. True, I had the contents of the micro-dot which could well be important, but all I had to do was give the papers and ring back to Jan when he turned up and that would be that. I paused, all the angles seemed to have been covered.

Then it hit me. What if he didn't turn up? There would be dangerous loose ends in the form of Zollenhorn and Luigi. Donetta was unpredictable and, without Jan, there was no one to stop her continuing to believe she could manipulate the situation in her favour. Lastly, I would be stuck with the micro-dot information, whatever that was.

As far as I could see, there was only one explanation for Jan going to see Harvac. Ivan's death had thrown him more than I had realized. He hadn't had time to calm down and he had gone there looking for revenge. If he was still there, he was in trouble and if he wasn't, why hadn't I heard from him?

I hadn't forgotten that he had saved me from Luigi giving me a bad beating, maybe worse. I owed him for that and, anyway, I couldn't just let things slide. The first thing to do was to go to the hotel and try to blag my way into getting a look around.

I put the photocopies and the ring back in the envelope, resealed it and addressed it to Isaac. I could post it to him when I went out. Then I wrote a note for Donetta telling her where I had gone. She might come back and, if she did, I wanted her to stay put. Next I had to work out a contingency plan and find someone to operate it. A quick mental run down of my list of friends left me with a very small selection team and only one serious choice. I phoned Claire.

19 THE HOTEL

The Dubrovnik hotel was about halfway down Belgrave Road, not far from Victoria Station. It was a large, cream painted building in a row of similar houses that were probably early nineteenth century. It had a glass door which opened on to a carpeted corridor leading past the stairs through to a breakfast room and lounge. The reception desk was in an alcove on the right as you went in. There was nothing on it but holiday leaflets and a brass bell. I hit the bell with an open palm and waited.

A small woman wearing a print pinafore over a black dress appeared from a door marked private and came slowly towards me. With tired movements, she opened the counter flap and went behind the desk.

"Can I help you?" She spoke with a strong East European accent.

"Yes, I would like to see Mr. Harvac. I am from a company called 'Golden Tours'. We arrange budget priced package holidays and I am researching suitable hotels for inclusion in some of our offers. This is just a preliminary inquiry to find out whether or not you would be interested and, if you are, the number of rooms, facilities offered, prices for block bookings - that sort of thing.

While I was talking, a smartly dressed girl with a suitcase battled with the glass door and struggled over to the counter. I glanced without recognition as Claire listened politely for a moment then, with exaggerated patience, picked up a leaflet and began to read.

I continued: "We have to be very selective about which hotels we use because, as you can imagine, for our deals to work they have to be a careful blend of customer satisfaction and cast iron costing."

The woman listened without interest and perhaps without comprehension.

"I go see if Mr. Harvac is in," she said, coming back out from behind the desk, "one moment please."

Claire smiled frostily and continued to study the leaflet. I looked at my watch like a man with a string of appointments and began to whistle soundlessly.

The first thing I noticed was the Armani suit, then

the open necked shirt and Gucci shoes, lastly I focused on a sallow, sardonic face and iron grey, wavy hair. The effect was on the rich side of sleazy, like a foreign fight promoter, until you saw the eyes. They were the eyes of a snake watching its prey.

"I believe you wanted to see me Mr. er..."

"Delaney, Peter Delaney."

We shook hands and Harvac, with a polite gesture, led the way down past the stairs to a room beyond the lounge. Behind me I heard Claire opening negotiations with the old lady for a room for the night.

The office was small and cluttered. A cheap desk, a phone, a computer and a fax filled most of the available space. A glass fronted bookcase with papers in it and on it and a few cardboard boxes took up the rest. A poster of Dubrovnik as seen from the sea and one of the Tower of London, mostly obscured by a beefeater, decorated the walls. Harvac sank into a battered swivel chair behind the desk and pointed to one of moulded plastic by the door. I pulled it over and sat down.

"I represent 'Golden Tours', Mr. Harvac..."

"Mr. Delaney, I won't put you to the trouble of continuing this nonsense. Miss Taveric has been here, we have made a deal and she is now going to do what she should have done some time ago."

"I see," I said. "I am really here because I am looking for a friend of mine who may have stayed here last night."

"Jan Kardelej? Yes, he is here. He has agreed to wait until Miss Taveric returns with my property."

"That's fine. I would like to have a word with him, if I may?"

"I am afraid not. No doubt he will contact you in due course. You have already wasted enough of my time. I must ask you to leave immediately."

"If I can't see him, you won't get the ring. I'm the only one who knows where it is."

Harvac's face didn't alter. He sighed and stood up.

"There are things besides the ring, " he said, "which Miss Taveric assures me she will be able to sort out. However, you can see Kardelej if you wish to. Taveric has another two hours to bring back the ring, after that I am sure you will want to help us. I hope, for your sake, that what you have just told me is true."

I didn't like the sound of that, but what could I do? I had to see Jan. Anyway, if things really got down and dirty, I could always give them the ring. I tried to tell myself that it wouldn't make any difference in the long run. After all, crime was a Hydra headed monster, you cut off one head and another grew in its place.

Harvac led the way. As we left the office, I saw a tall man standing outside with his hands behind his back who looked to me like an ex-soldier. I remembered Rimbaud's line, 'I was of the race that sang under torture'. I knew what he meant.

We went up in an old rickety lift as far as the fourth floor and then took the stairs to a narrow, uncarpeted landing that hadn't been painted in a long time. Staff accommodation, I thought. With out a word, Harvac unlocked one of the doors, waved me in and locked it behind me.

The room was also uncarpeted. There was a tiny sink with a mirror above it, a chest of drawers, a chair, a small wooden table and an iron frame single bed. Jan was lying on the bed. I went over to wake him, winced, closed my eyes and turned away. My stomach heaved. His throat had been cut from ear to ear.

After a few moments, I forced myself to look closer. All I could see was the wide gaping gash, like a red madman's smile. There wasn't much blood, so I knew he had been killed somewhere else and brought here. I took a folded blanket from under his feet at the end of the bed and covered him up. I thought that would help, somehow make him more decent, but it didn't. That gaping wound and those shocked, staring eyes still lingered in my mind.

I went over to the sink and splashed cold water on my face, drying it with a bald, worn out towel. I liked Jan, or had liked him. It was difficult to put him in the past. Even now, I wouldn't have been surprised if the figure on the bed had somehow come to life. I was still numb with shock. Two words kept going round in my mind in a meaningless mantra, stupidity and waste, stupidity and waste. Suddenly, my feelings unlocked in an explosion of blind rage. I rushed over to the door and started kicking it with my boot.

"Harcac!" I yelled, "Come up here, you stupid bastard. I'll break you in two you useless tub of lard. You hear me Harvac? Harvac!..."

I stopped to listen, waiting for the footstep on the stair, the rattle of the key in the door, but there was nothing. Silence. No one came, no one went. All I could hear was the somnambulant quiet of a hotel at mid-day.

Then, as quickly as it had come, my anger drained away to be replaced by fear. I turned from the door and started to pace the room, ever aware of Jan's silent presence. The wider connotations of the situation had begun to sink in. Now that I knew about Jan, there was no way they were going to let me walk off into the sunset and when Donetta failed to come up with the ring, they would use gentle persuasion to get me to talk before they killed me. On top of that, there was Claire to worry about.

I had been fairly sure that Jan was being held against his will, so the plan had been for me to track him down and then, if possible, to get him out. Claire's role was to have been to provide a room we could hide Jan in if necessary, or to go to the police if I got into difficulties. It all seemed a little loose now, but in the safety of my own kitchen it had looked foolproof and also not dangerous for Claire. My only hope was that she would go straight to the police when I didn't appear and not waste time looking for me. Meanwhile, I had to try and get myself out.

The room was in the attic of the hotel and the one window was cut into the side of the roof. Below this was a gully which ran between the foot of the roof and the raised lip of the wall. The window was small, but maybe I could crawl through it, make my way along the gully to the end of the building, and jump to the neighbouring one. If I had had a grappling hook and a rope and if I had been an Alpine climber or a member of the S.A.S. I might have managed it. As it was, I didn't fancy my chances. The only other way out was through the door and breaking that down would take time and maybe a sledge hammer.

Two light taps interrupted my train of thought. I stopped to listen. They came again. I walked over to the door.

"Yes?"

"It's Claire."

"How did you find me?"

"I am on the fourth floor. I saw you going up here with that man. Is Jan with you?"

"Jan is dead. Did you bring the tools?"

"I brought my bicycle kit and a hack saw."

"Give me the screwdriver from the kit, it's flat and will slide under the door. What number room are you in?"

"403."

"Go back and wait for me and for Christ's sake don't let anyone see you."

Luckily, I was on the inside of the door. There were four screws holding the lock on. I cleaned off the paint and unscrewed the lock. The door opened. The stairs were almost immediately opposite, not more than six or seven feet away. I listened. A stair board creaked. One of the staff was going to his room, or somebody was coming to check on me. I waited. A head appeared above the level of the floor behind the banister railings. It was the soldier.

I launched myself across the landing, hitting him in the chest. We both crashed down the stairs with me on top and him clawing the air, desperately trying to save himself. His head hit the wall at the bottom with the force of both our weights behind it. He went as limp as a dead rabbit. I disentangled myself and climbed to my feet, my knee was killing me. I looked down, there was a tear in my jeans and blood on my leg. I must have cut it on a nail during the fall.

I stood for a moment expecting the roof to cave in. A vacuum cleaner rumbled on the floor below and a siren sounded lazily in the distance, but the wrecking crew stayed put, buried too far away in the bowels of the hotel to know the difference. I limped along to 403 and Claire let me in.

"What was that noise?" she said, as she shut the door.

"I bumped into one of Harvac's men. He's out cold, but we don't have long, five minutes, maybe ten, before someone goes to look for him, or he comes round. No one knows we are connected, so you can walk out and get the police now. I will wait here. Unless they start searching the rooms immediately, I will be safe enough until you get back."

For a second she hesitated, not wanting to run out on me, then she grabbed her bag.

"I'll be as quick as I can," she said, "here take this."

She dipped her hand into her bag and pulled out a silver automatic.

"Where did you get that?" I said. I could hardly believe my luck.

She pointed it at me and fired. A small flame appeared at the end of the barrel.

"It's a cigarette lighter," she explained, "it was the nearest thing to a weapon I had in the house."

"Thanks," I said, slipping it into my pocket, "I

might run out of matches while you're gone."

She smiled apologetically, put her bag on her shoulder and slowly opened the door. From the other side a hand pushed it wider. Surprised, she stepped back. Harvac walked into the room with a gun in his hand.

20 HARVAC

"Most residents don't leave blood outside their doors," he said, "but it was a good attempt Delaney, I hadn't given you credit for that much brain."

"You can't get away with killing us," I said. The line sounded jaded and lame, even to me. "Too many people know we are here."

"I doubt that," he replied, "but it wouldn't matter if they did. There will be no traces."

"We are not in some isolated wood in Eastern Europe," I said, "this is London. Do you really think you can get rid of three bodies and no questions asked?"

Harvac's eyes twinkled, to him it was like watching dead meat talking and it amused him.

"Easily," he laughed, "so easily I don't feel it is clever anymore. You see your world is illusory and illusions can be made to come and go. You think that here we are standing in the middle of a well ordered machine called Society composed of Law, Justice, Moral Responsibility, Etiquette etc. and that this enables human life to function. Pah!" He made a dismissive movement with his hand. "That is all a sham, a facade beneath which the primeval beat of the real world moves unfettered. Lust, Greed, Fear, push one of those buttons and you can control anyone - understand those rhythms and you have power. Humanity is not moving in chaos alleviated by law as you dreamers think, it is moving in ever more easily controlled order to those three simple emotions. People like Kardelej and his father hoped to build a new Croatia, but while they have been hoping and talking, we have gone ahead and made a new Europe - one that knows which side its bread is buttered and one that co-operates very well across all borders. No, I don't think many questions will be asked."

"You left out vanity," I said. "But you have forgotten that I have your new Europe on paper."

The gun moved slightly to point more directly at Claire.

"Delaney," he said, "over the last few days you have been the subject of much study. Why were you involved? What did you hope to gain? What was your angle? Finally, we worked it out. Nothing. No angle. You were merely a sentimental fool with a crazy English idea of fair play who believed anything a beautiful woman told him. So far, that has made you a wild card whose reactions were difficult to predict. Not any more, I now trust you implicitly."

"What do you mean?"

"I mean you will tell me where the information is because, if you don't, I will shoot this girl in say - ten seconds."

"Wait! You don't have to shoot anybody." I put a note of desperation into my voice. It wasn't hard. "I have the ring here."

Spreading my hands wide to show my pacific intentions, I slowly dug one hand into the pocket of my jeans and came up with Donetta's other ring. Harvac relaxed fractionally and smiled. I tossed it over to him a little to one side of his body. His left hand deftly snatched it out of the air as I dived for his gun arm, grabbing it with both hands and forcing it inwards and upwards. There was an explosion and Harvac fell backwards. The bullet had gone in under his chin and out through the top of his head. Dark blood and brain oozed on to the carpet. I knelt down and prized the gun from between his fingers.

"Come on," I said, "let's go."

I stepped out into the corridor holding Claire by the hand. The first thing I saw was the soldier. He was walking slowly towards me, obviously still in no condition for fast thinking. He must have heard the shot and expected to see Harvac. His face showed surprise, then, fear, as he became aware of the gun and the way I must have looked. By this time, I was so far gone I would have taken on the marines. He half raised his hands and stood back, waiting to be shot. We went past him in silence and when I got my last glimpse of him as we ran down the stairs, he hadn't moved.

We slowed down as we came to the ground floor. I tucked the gun into the belt of my jeans at the back where it would be covered by my jacket. The old woman was dozing behind the desk. I hoped we would get past without waking her. No such luck. She saw us and some intuition immediately told her we were the agents of tragedy. She came out from the desk at us screaming curses in Croatian. I got between Claire and her clawing fingers and holding her at arms length to keep her nails away from my eyes, we made it out the door in an undignified scramble. As we went down the steps to the street, her voice turned to low, muttered moaning behind us. It occurred to me that she was probably Harvac's mother, and the thought of her seeing him lying in that room with half his head blown off gave didn't make me feel any better.

21 GILES'S PLACE

I hailed the first taxi I saw and told the driver to go to Redcliffe Gardens. My place was out of the question, even Claire's was too risky. I had to stay out of the way until I could get the stuff from Isaac when the post arrived the next morning, then I could go to the police. If I went without the evidence to back up my story, I would probably be the one to go down for murder. They would be confronted by two dead bodies and a homicidal maniac - me. I would make an anonymous phone call as soon as I could and hope the police got there in time to find Jan and Harvac. In the meantime I had to get hold of Donetta, I did not want her to go back to the hotel before she knew what had happened.

I paid the taxi off in Redcliffe Gardens and we walked along to a dilapidated house on the corner. I opened a gate in the railings and we went down the steps to a basement flat. The great de Rais opened to my knock and imperiously waved us in. The front room was dark with a curtain across the barred window. There was a double divan bed against the opposite wall covered with a black duvet. His guitar was lying across it. Two candles burned on either side of a small statue of Dionysus in the centre of the mantelpiece above a closed fire place. There was a cheap desk in the inset next to it. A sofa, a table and the door took up all the space on the third wall. Two sets of shelves containing books, cd's and a music system stood on either side of the window. A print of Richard Dadd's 'The Fairy feller's Masterstroke' was pinned to the wall. Holst's 'Planets' wafted from the speakers.

I sat down on the chair at his desk, Claire sank into the sofa. Giles followed us into the room pushing his hair away from his eyes.

"Where's Donetta?" he asked in the aggrieved tone of a man who had given me something to look after which I had carelessly lost.

"That is what I want you to find out," I replied.

"The last I heard from Isaac was that she and you had disappeared into the midnight accompanied by some weirdo army type."

"The weirdo army type is dead. Claire and I have just escaped from the hotel where he was murdered and if we don't find Donetta, she could be next on the list. There is a chance she could be contacted through one of her friends at the Noire and that is where you come in. We can't risk being seen, but you could go round there and check it out. Watch yourself and don't tell anyone we are here."

He accepted this without comment. He lived so much in his own world that he had long since given up trying to make sense of his occasional brushes with reality.

"OK I will go round there now. Help yourselves to tea or coffee. I don't think there is much food, but you are welcome to whatever you can find."

The word food reminded me of how hungry I was and, as I knew the contents of his larder would threaten a mouse with starvation, I pulled out a twenty pound note and gave it to him.

"Pick up some sandwiches and a bottle of wine on your way back," I said, "we haven't eaten since breakfast. And be careful."

"Trust me, man. I will be discreet, a ghost gliding through London's meanest streets."

He put on his red velvet jacket, tied his green and

yellow silk scarf loosely round his neck and left to go round the corner to the Old Brompton Road.

After he had gone, I took the gun from my belt where it had been digging into my spine and put it on the desk. Then I went across the square to a public telephone box and reported Jan's and Harvac's deaths. I didn't use Giles' phone in case they managed to trace the call. When I got back Claire had made some coffee and we sat down to wait. I was still trying to come to terms with Jan's murder.

"I can't believe he would have gone there if he thought he would be recognized," I said. "Donetta must have turned up at the hotel with some crazy idea of doing a deal with Harvac and somehow blown Jan's cover."

"If she did, it would have been by accident or coercion, they seem to have been friends for a while."

"You are right. That is why she agreed to get the ring, she was trying to save Jan's life."

A half an hour later, Giles returned swinging a carrier bag containing sandwiches and a bottle of wine.

"No sign of Donetta, and she hasn't contacted

Pascal or Leo."

An idea struck me. She would have gone back to the flat, if Jan had told her he had sent the ring there, or even if he hadn't, it was the first place she would look. It was just possible that she was dumb enough to be still there.

"I had better try my place," I said, reaching for the phone on the desk. I let it ring for a long time while watching Giles lay out the sandwiches and open the wine. Finally, someone picked it up.

"Donetta! get out of there fast and go to the police. Ring me from the station and I'll come over."

"She won't go to the police and neither will you, Delaney - unless you want to be charged with murder. You cannot survive long unless I help you. Let's meet."

I slammed down the phone and stood up.

"Luigi's at the flat," I said, "and he knows about Harvac. He is probably going through my papers now, which means somebody could be round here very soon."

Claire looked at me in shock, a sandwich half way to her mouth. Giles was munching studiously and alternately sipping wine as if he hadn't heard me. He looked like a man who hadn't eaten all day. I grabbed a glass of wine, got it down in one and poured myself another, lighting a cigarette to go with it.

"Are you sure you saw no one suspicious at the Noire?" Claire asked Giles.

"No one I noticed. A little fat guy left at the same time as I did, but I saw him go into a phone box before I went in to the delicatessen to get the sandwiches and he had gone when I came out."

I remembered that night at Clapham Common station and the man who had followed me. The description fitted. I would have taken bets that this was the same man. I tried to phone Isaac to warn him, but there was no answer. Without access to my flat I couldn't even tell if he was out at a gig. I had no way of tracking him down. I could only hope he would be back home by morning.

I gave myself full marks for telling Giles to check out the Noire. If there was a wrong move to make, I made it. Now I had to think of some way of getting us out without leaving him holding the baby - and it had to be quick, before the fat man could get hold of some back up.

"I'll go and see if he is outside," I said.

"Don't," cried Claire, "he can't know for certain

we are here. There must be another way out - isn't there, Giles?"

"My neighbour's flat goes through to the back garden, but she's away," he replied, "we could try and break in, of course."

"No," I said, "I won't be in danger while they think they can get the micro-dot information out of me. Whatever happens, don't react."

I picked up the gun and handed it to Giles.

"Here, hide this."

I gave him what I hoped was a confident smile and went out of the flat and up the steps to the street. The man in the raincoat was strolling along with his hands in his pockets, an innocent citizen without a care in the world. I don't quite know what I had in mind, maybe I thought I could talk him into letting us go, maybe I was hoping he wouldn't be there. Whatever it was it all went out the window. The tension and fear of the last few days had got to me and I completely lost it. I flung my arms around him from behind, pinning his arms to his sides. He was smaller than me so I think I had some crazy idea of dragging him down into the flat, but it didn't work. Using my momentum, he bent forward, twisting sharply at the same time. I felt myself sliding over his right shoulder and the next thing I knew I was on my back on the pavement in front of him. A big black automatic had appeared in his hand and it was pointing at my head.

"Still playing silly buggers Delaney. Let's get off the street before someone asks you for an autograph."

I got to my feet, dusted myself off and led the way back down the steps. Before we reached the door, Giles had opened it with a 'what's all this about' expression on his face. I gave him a blank look and we went into the front room. I sat on the sofa beside Claire, Giles sat on the bed, the fat man stood in front of the fire place, holding the automatic easily and professionally, not pointing it at anybody. With his free hand he took a plastic wallet from his inside pocket and tossed it in my direction.

"Jones, Interpol," he said, "take a butcher's."

I flicked open the wallet and saw an identification card with a chubby faced photograph of him, a number and the word Interpol printed on it. I closed it and spun it back to him.

"Looks all right." I said.

"I have been following the trail of various objets d'arts that have been finding their way on to the

European and American markets from Eastern Europe. A lot of this stuff is stolen, some of it is fake and most of it seems to go through the hands of Michael Zollenhorn and his partner, Luigi Sorelli. You came in to the frame after Sorelli visited you at your flat. You checked clear, but that don't mean nothing in this business. I had you down as a possible mule and when you linked up with Voinavitch in Paris that seemed to clinch it. I have been hanging around for the last couple of days because I know from my contacts at Oakwood that you're in some sort of trouble with Zollenhorn and a man in trouble needs help and a man who needs help gives help."

"How can I help you?"

"My prime targets are Zollenhorn and Sorelli - you can help me nail them."

"I don't know much that could be of use and most of that is guess work, but tomorrow I am getting hold of some information that could really make a difference."

His expression didn't change, but the gun seemed to point more directly at me.

"Why tomorrow?

"I posted it to myself this morning to keep it out

of circulation. It should arrive between eight and nine tomorrow. The only problem is Luigi Sorelli is there at the moment. I don't know how long he intends to stay.

"That's no problem, I'll get some of the local boys to pick him up. Mind if I use your phone?"

"Not at all," said Giles, "and how about a glass of wine to celebrate. I don't know what this is all about but I can tell you Pete has been going through it. The planets must have been out of alignment and he won't carry a crystal no matter how often I tell him, but now you are here God's in his heaven and all's right with the world - as Browning would say."

While he was talking, Giles had picked up the nearly empty bottle of wine and a glass and was proffering them to Jones with a childishly happy grin on his face. Jones, who had put the gun on the desk in order to tap out the number declined brusquely while concentrating on waiting for someone to pick up the phone. Someone answered just as Giles brought the bottle down so hard on his head that it smashed. Jones crumpled awkwardly to the floor between the chair and the desk, the receiver sliding from his hand. Giles picked it up, replaced it on the handset and turned towards us.

"You weren't falling for that bullshit, were you?" he said.

"If he is innocent," I replied, "you're looking at one to three years, if not, you are probably in line for a George Cross."

I jumped to my feet and pulled the fallen man out straight on the floor and made sure nothing was interrupting his breathing.

"He mentioned Voinavitch's icon," I continued, "he couldn't have known about that unless Voinavitch or Zollenhorn had told him. Call an ambulance, tell them he fell down your steps, probably drunk, then lose yourself until tomorrow morning. Once we have those papers everything can be sorted out."

Five minutes later we left the flat and walked down to Earls Court tube station. We took the train to Russell Square where we booked into a hotel.

22 FINAL MEETING

Isaac's tousled head appeared out of the window and looked down.

"Oh it's you," he said, "I suppose you had better come up."

It was seven thirty in the morning, sharp and cold with a touch of early winter frost. Claire and I had been rattling on Isaac's door for a good three minutes. He let us in and led the way up the dark staircase to his room. The first thing I saw was Donetta coming out of the kitchen annex carrying a pot of tea and two mugs. She didn't seem surprised to see me. I introduced her to Claire while Isaac came up with two more mugs. I explained why we had come to wake him up so early.

"The post usually gets here about eight thirty," he said, pouring out four strong teas.

We sat round the table and for a few moments

there was silence, then Donetta looked across at me.

"You can't have the stuff, Pete," she said, quietly.

"No? How did you find out it was coming here?"

"When I saw your note at the flat, I knew you wouldn't have taken it with you and you didn't have many other options open to you in the time. This was the most obvious one. I came over here and persuaded Isaac to let me stay."

I didn't say anything. I could feel Harvac's gun hard against my spine. I had tucked it into my jeans before we left the hotel. Claire was looking into her tea cup as if it had her undivided attention, but I knew she would accept no substitutes, once we got those lists, the next stop was the police and that was that. Isaac was noisily buttering a slice if toast. Finally, Donetta said: "I made a deal with Harvac."

"For the ring," I sneered.

"For Jan," she replied.

"Don't give me that," I said, "Jan's dead and you know it."

She looked at me for a second in horrified disbelief, then her eyes filled with tears and she began to cry.

Claire was round the table in a second and put her arm round her shoulders.

"Pete thought you knew," she said, "or he wouldn't have told you like that. I'm sorry."

"The cruel, calculating bastard," she sobbed, "he gave me his word."

"It wan't your fault," I said, "Jan should not have gone over there. He was thrown by Ivan's murder."

"No," said Donetta, "it is my fault, if I hadn't gone to see Harvac, he might still be alive.

"Tell us what happened"

"After our argument, I was furious with you for refusing to help me. I went over to see Harvac and told him we knew about the micro-dot and that my uncle should have informed me about what it was I was delivering. I said I had no interest in his secret messages, but the ring was mine. He said my stupidity had caused them a lot of unnecessary trouble, but, as I was Taveric's niece, I could keep the ring as long as I gave him what he wanted. Of course I didn't have it and I had to tell him about Jan, although I didn't mention his name. It didn't seem to be a dangerous thing to do. I never dreamed that Jan could actually be in the hotel at the time. He was, though, and he must have seen me or heard me or something, because he was suddenly in the office beside me.

'Come on, Donetta,' he said, 'let's go.'

"Harvac went for a gun in a desk drawer, but Jan was quicker and covered him with his gun while putting me behind him with his other hand. We them started to back out the door. Harvac didn't move, he just watched us, but he must have pressed a button with his foot or something because suddenly a huge hand grabbed me by the hair and jerked me backwards into the corridor. I screamed and Jan spun round but he didn't shoot in case he hit me, even after what I had just done to him. The guy fired round me and hit Jan in the arm, making him drop his gun. The next second Harvac had knocked Jan to the floor and the two of them were standing over him with their guns stuck in his face. I was sure they were going to kill him.

'Wait!' I screamed, 'He won't have anything on him. If you let him go, I will get it for you.'

"Harvac stepped back.

'OK' he said, 'bring it here and I will let both of you go. I don't want any unnecessary trouble. You have got twenty-four hours.'

She started to cry again.

"I should have known he would never let Jan go, once he had got hold of him. Everything he stood for, honesty, belief, justice, made him hateful to a grubby, corrupt, manipulator like Harvac. I will kill him." She spoke the last words in a simple, matter-of-fact way, to no one in particular, but they had a deadly finality.

"You won't have to," I said, glad to be able to distract her from her grief, "he is already dead."

I told her how Claire and I had discovered Jan's body and then escaped from the hotel, killing Harvac in the process. As she listened, a smile of unholy joy transformed her face and she drank in every word as if it had the sweet taste of nectar, the nectar of revenge.

"That leaves the organisation," she said, "Jan was right, these people must be stopped."

At that moment, there came a slap from the letterbox below. Isaac leapt for the door and clattered downstairs, returning with my large brown envelope. He handed it to me.

"We are going to Marylebone Police Station now," I said to Donetta, "it might be helpful if you came too."

"Of course," she said.

She followed us downstairs, I unlocked the door and we stepped out into Daventry Street. A cold sun, low in the south east, angling over the houses opposite had already turned some of the patches of frost into dampness. The street was empty and we started walking towards Bell Street. Suddenly, Luigi and Zollenhorn came round the corner. They were about twenty yards away and moving quickly. The time for negotiation had passed. I saw Luigi's arm swing upwards holding a heavy forty five automatic. I dropped the envelope and fumbled desperately for the Mauser under my jacket. Donetta screamed and jumped in front of me just as Luigi's gun crashed twice. Donetta spun backwards like a leaf caught in a gust of wind. I had the gun out now, shock had numbed me into a sense of unreality. It felt like a childhood game. I stepped sideways, flicked the safety off with my thumb, fired and kept firing. The gun felt light in my hands, the shots sounded lighter than I expected. Luigi staggered and then stumbled. One bullet hit him in the eye. I saw the blood spurt out. Then he was down. His body convulsed and shuddered for a moment and lay still.

I stopped firing, the magazine was empty and had been for the last five or six times I squeezed the trigger. Zollenhorn was running back the way he had come, a paunchy figure with a mission, his own personal safety. I threw the gun away and turned. Claire was kneeling beside Donetta trying to staunch the bleeding with a handkerchief. Isaac was leaning out of his window shouting that an ambulance and the police were on their way. Donetta was lying quietly staring at the sky. I could see a wound in her shoulder and one below her left breast. Her blouse and Claire's handkerchief were soaked in blood. A strange half smile seemed to tug at the corners of her mouth when she saw me. She tried to say something, but no words came. By the time the police arrived, thirty seconds later, she was dead.

The list turned out to be quite useful to the police both here and in Europe, although only a few of the politicians were prosecuted, including Taveric. Jan, at least, had achieved his object. I don't know what happened to the ring, I think it might have gone to an Austrian museum. Donetta and Jan were sent back to Croatia and given a hero's funeral by their friends, Ivan was never found.

It did not take Giles long to resume his visits, but if there were anymore mysterious girls around he kept them to himself. I didn't mind, Claire provided all the mystery I could handle.

ABOUT THE AUTHOR

James Flynn is a musician and writer. He has published three other books, "The Blues Play Herbie Watson", 'The Elf and the Witch", and "Songs and Poems". With his brother, Nick, he has recorded two CDs, "The Flynn Brothers" and "Duo". He is married and lives in London.